Daringly DifferOnt

AfrO-Centric ShOrt StOries

Daringly DifferOnt

AfrO-Centric
ShOrt StOries

BY
m. i. williams jr.

M.I. Williams Jr.

Daringly DifferOnt AfrO-Centric ShOrt StOries

Published by Spines

ISBN:979-8-90002-875-0

Spines

Table of Contents

Introduction vii

Acknowledgements ix

1. The Necklace 1

2. The Floating Flowers of Hilton Head Island 9

3. A Second Chance 15

4. The Curious Curse of Carol Stanton-White 25

5. WHITE MEAT 35

6. Another Sunny Southern California Day 45

7. The Reef 59

8. Transformation 67

9. Mrs. Dinwitty's Herbal Tea 79

10. A Washington State Love Story 87

Introduction

Writing is always deeply personal and yet unavoidably public. Writing is truly artistic in the sense that the writer doesn't want anyone to see or share in the piece until it is absolutely perfect. To allow a stranger to share in one's most personal thoughts and ideas of a story opens up the writer to possible criticism, misunderstanding, rejection, and even failure as a creator. But a committed writer has no choice but to risk it all because it is a calling and a passion. All the stories within were birthed from my passion to write, to entertain, to share some of my personal experiences that I have been able to weave into these stories. Every story has some grain of truth as well as an imaginative dose of "what if." I have met many of the characters that you will meet, and as you will see, they have left an indelible imprint upon me. Have I ever met Mrs. Dinwitty? Yes—often, in various Black churches. Or do I really know the addictively beautiful Carol Stanton-White? Yes, I do. What I suspect is that you too have met many of my characters but in your own social settings. Many African-Americans will easily recognize many of my characters because they are our neighbors, grandmothers, and friends.

I have merely tried to present a minute slice and taste of the greater and vastly broader Afro-centric experience.

So sit back, or curl up in your most comfortable reading position, and start your journey into my world—the world of

Daringly Differ0nt Afr0-Centric Sh0rt St0ries.

Acknowledgements

First, let me thank my family for their patience in indulging me in my passion, especially my daughter Kira Lynne, for being my vigilant unofficial editor.

A special thanks to my mother, Mrs. Gwendolyn E. Sitgraves, for always exhorting me "to go for it!"

My friend Cheryl B. and my son Marcus III, for sharing their circumstances and stories with me and allowing me to share them with others.

And finally, Mrs. Patricia C. McKissack, storyteller and writer extraordinaire, whose book, The Dark Thirty: Southern Tales of the Supernatural, inspired me (unknowingly) to turn my ideas and experiences into these stories.

Thank you all.
m. i. williams jr.

The Necklace

(a short story by m. i. williams jr.)

Its origins remain a mystery even today. For those who have encountered its power, it has been seen simultaneously as both a curse and a blessing. But no one who has had it come into their lives can deny that their lives have been forever altered. Its beauty is in the intricate pattern of its creative design. It begs to be touched, held, worn, owned. A dark silver chain with a medallion of what appears to be the symbol of the crucified Savior.

A beaming bright cross that symbolizes the death not only of Jesus, the Christ, but also the transforming death of hatred, envy, lies, and especially evil earthly thoughts. How often do Christians wear the symbol of their resurrected Savior, only to daily do and think things that represent the very opposite of what it symbolizes? Perhaps this was the sole purpose for the necklace's creation. Perhaps the necklace was created to make its wearer worthy of the man that died on the real cross.

Margaret Hudson was a deaconess at the Glenville Baptist Missionary Church. She enjoyed attending church. She enjoyed it because her husband Arthur was the head deacon. Arthur was also a successful store owner in the Black community.

This afforded Margaret a lofty status that no one would have dared question in the church or the community. She spent hours shopping for the right clothes that would reinforce her position in the community, especially when it came to her accessories—her shoes, hats, and above all, her jewelry.

It was therefore understandable that when Mother Brown died, Margaret was bequeathed her favorite hats and even the beautiful dark silver necklace that everyone secretly coveted. And now it was hers!

What pleased her even more was the thought that Mother Brown had bequeathed it to her on her deathbed. She decided that she would show it off on first Sunday when she would be attired in her deaconess white dress. Margaret ran her fingers over it again and again. It felt smooth to the touch. She wanted to put it on but instinctively knew nothing would bespeak its beauty until she had just the right clothes to match its grandeur.

Sunday arrived, and Deaconess Hudson donned the coveted jewelry. It hung perfectly around her caramel neck. As she walked down the aisle, she glanced to see who was looking at her. Sister Pratt gave an approving grin, as if to say, "Go girl, you know you lookin' good." Likewise, Sister Mapp gave an admiring look.

However, when it came to Sister Dorothy Smyth, who

resisted any kind of outward flamboyancy, she conspicuously bowed her head and began to pray.

Sister Hudson thought to herself, "Old stick in the mud, that's why you ain't got no man now. Never did a thing to get a man to notice you." Just then, Sister Hudson received a stabbing pain at the back of her neck. She jerked so violently that the usher who was leading her to her seat asked if she was ok. Regaining her composure, Sister Hudson just smiled. During the sermon, Sister Hudson became bored and allowed her mind to wander. She paused at the choir loft. That Yolanda had sure grown up, she thought. She was even getting a little hippy—maybe it just appeared that way because she wore her clothes so tight. **"Please God, don't let her get pregnant."** Just then, the necklace yanked around her throat like a dog choker! Sister Hudson yelled out, "Jesus! Have mercy, Lord!" Someone yelled out, "Ain't he alright? Give in to the Spirit, Sister Hudson." In a flash, the Nurse's Aide women were on Sister Hudson with fans and holding her hands, which surely stopped her from trying to yank the necklace off. Being a rather astute woman, Sister Hudson began putting two and two together.

After pretending to regain her composure and holding one finger up to heaven, Sister Hudson marched up the aisle, through the vestibule, and straight into the Ladies Lounge. Stealing away into the first available stall, she grabbed at the clasp of the necklace.

As if out of a scene from The Wizard of Oz, when she tried to undo the necklace, it emitted a hot white electrical charge that caused Sister Hudson to yell out. Luckily, no one was in earshot. The necklace was now quite hot and uncomfortable around her neck. Sister Hudson began to panic and cry. "Oh Lord, help me please! I get it! Please stop this torture and I will do better!" Instantly, the heat abated, so much so that it seemed to emit a soothing coolness. Calmly, Sister Hudson again tried to release the clasp, and again the necklace gave a shock—but this time substantially milder. For now, the necklace and she were inseparable. Sister Hudson left the lounge and sat stressed out and bewildered in the vestibule for the rest of the service, with a Nurse's Aide hovering by, just in case.

On the drive home, Arthur inquired if she was alright. He had never seen his super cool wife respond to the Spirit in church like that before. Not wanting to lie, she merely smiled faintly and didn't answer.

Arthur smiled back, not knowing where to take the conversation next because Margaret always had an opinion and an answer for everything... but not today. Arthur, wanting to please his wife, ended the one-sided conversation by complimenting his wife: "You know you really looked stunning today in your new dress and that gorgeous necklace." Margaret mustered a meek "thank you."

Over the next few weeks, Margaret Hudson became quite introspective. She was purposely conscious of her thoughts and attitudes. She began to take stock of her life. It was a very good life by the standards of the community. But Margaret began to see that her life was solely all about herself. She had borne Arthur only one son because she didn't want to become fat and matronly. True, she was a good homemaker, but not once had she ever gone to the store to help Arthur. She went only when she had a need.

As she intermittently reviewed her life, she further saw that she was quite self-centered and vain. She did only the things that brought her attention and compliments from people that she really didn't even like. Through it all, Arthur had loved her. She reflected on how kind he was, not just to her but to everyone. And everyone seemed to genuinely like him. Margaret became aware that it was she who was the lucky one in their marriage, not Arthur.

Margaret noticed that she tended to think these insightful thoughts when she was stroking the necklace. Since it never came off, she hid it with various types of clothing and scarves. But after a while, it became a part of her. In her effort to become a better Christian, better wife, and a better person, Margaret Hudson began to earnestly devote herself to Jesus by helping those less fortunate than she. The Union Station food bank saw her as a regular donor and volunteer. She gave most of her fancy clothes to the **Second Chance for Women** group that helped women look for work.

She also began to help Arthur regularly at the store by counting and storing the inventory. Gradually, she began to feel good about herself, not with the old vain-glory, but as someone who felt useful. She no longer had time to think about the frailties or shortcomings of others. She indeed was modeling the noble character of a Christian woman, and everyone seemed to notice, especially Arthur.

One evening, as she was leaving the store, she noticed an unfamiliar man hovering near her. As she turned to get into the car, he grabbed her and violently pushed her into the side alley. A knife appeared out of nowhere, and he demanded her cash or her life!

Margaret replied with a confidence and courage that the "would-be thief" had not expected: "I have no money to give you. All I have to give you is the advice that you need Jesus!"

The thief knew she was telling the truth about the money and about Jesus. But not wanting to go away empty-handed, he replied, "Yeah ok, but that necklace is coming with me!" Pushing her hard against the brick building, he aggressively grabbed the necklace.

It was then that the necklace discharged a continuous blue light of power that burned the hand of the thief so badly that his hand smelled like burned bacon! Margaret, on the other hand, felt absolutely nothing. Unable to release the scorching object, the thief cried out to Margaret to make it stop. She yelled back, "I can't!" On his knees, with his hands still clenching the electrifying necklace, he cried out to her: "Help me please! I'm sorry lady... please!"

Margaret closed her eyes and spoke aloud. "Lord, I think that he's learned his lesson. Have pity on him for Jesus' sake." Instantly, the charge ceased. The thief sobbed and held his hand ever so gingerly. After a period of recuperation, the 'would-be thief" spoke, "Youz one of God's chosen, aint' you? I'm sorry, truly I am. I swear, I swear, I'll never thieve again. NEVER!

Thank you! Thank you!" As he hobbled away, Margaret saw him hurl the knife down the gutter.

Margaret didn't tell what happened to her to anyone. She was now convinced that God had indeed used the necklace to infuse her with a new insight... a Godly insight. She now understood that Mother Brown saw something that needed to be fixed within her that only the necklace could accomplish.

She was no longer afraid of it. She now saw it more like Moses' staff—the rod of correction that Pharaoh needed.

Another first Sunday came and Margaret Hudson was in her seat early before the crowd arrived. She no longer needed to be seen. She wanted only to thank God for keeping her and showing her the way to being a better Christian. At the end of service, two curious things happened.

First, Arthur came down the front aisle to testify before the entire church. Margaret listened intently to his words. "Church," he said, "I've been blessed by God. His promises are true. Psalm 1 says that whatever a righteous man does it will be fruitful. But I need to thank my God not for my business, nor my status, not for my house, nor anything material. Today I just want God and ya'll to know that my greatest blessing is my wife.

She is a woman of noble character, and should I **die** tonight, I want her to know that this man loves and cherishes her above any and all earthly things." "I love you, Margaret." There wasn't a dry eye in the house—especially those of Margaret.

As the Hudsons were leaving, who should come up to them but Sister Roberta Goodwin, the wife of Dr. Charles Goodwin, in all her usual silvery finery. "Arthur, that was a beautiful testimony about your wife. And everyone knows she is one of the finest-dressing women in town, especially with that necklace. Margaret, when you get tired of it, you KNOW you can give it to me." Margaret instinctively touched the necklace, and it fell unexpectedly into her hand. She smiled. "Now that you mention it Sister Roberta, I think this necklace would do you some good. Take it and consider it a gift."

Sister Goodwin couldn't believe her eyes or ears. Margaret reassured her, "Seriously! Take it, it's yours!" "Thank you, Girl!" replied Sister Goodwin. As Margaret got into the car, she turned to Sister Goodwin and responded, "Don't mention it... wearing it will make you feel like a new woman."

The Floating Flowers of Hilton Head Island

(a short story by m.i. williams jr.)

Hilton Head Island is nature's way of showing off. Everywhere the eye looks, there is stunning beauty... and it has always been that way. As far back as the Reconstruction Era, every visitor who has come to the shoe-shaped island found that they've left a little bit of their soul on its beaches or its hidden meadows. Exotic birds, fish, and unusual aquatic amphibians had always been in abundance in this picturesque garden of nature. Is it any wonder why many a freed slave and free Negro rushed to Hilton Head when General Mitchel of the victorious Union Army set aside a portion of the north side of the island for the ex-slaves and their kin? So thankful were these people that they named the town Mitchelville.

Mitchelville was a place of peace, tranquility, and proportional beauty. Even the marshes and swamps seemed manicured. The residents of Mitchelville slowly began to prosper from the rich growing soil and successful husbandry. One of the most successful farmers was Thaddeus Standborne.

His land included not only part of a rich marsh, but also prime farmland, pasture, and a serene lake that he shared generously with his neighbors; permitting them to swim and fish from sun-up to sundown during the summer months. But Thaddeus' greatest joy was not his success. That joy was his family. Thad's parents had always been free. He was well read and had received formal training in the army as a supply officer which made him valuable to the struggling southern whites during and briefly after the war. In truth, he had been the only local liaison that the army had recognized and trusted. This last fact was an onerous pill to swallow for some of the old white guard who had lost much of their power, status, and influence in the new order. This deep-seated resentment would play itself out in the course of time. Thad had three wonderful children by Sadie Demus. He had seen Sadie hanging wash for her struggling mistress when she smiled at him. He knew right then that she was special and he pursued her and secured her freedom before the year ended.

Thad invested quality time with his children.

He took time to teach them everything he knew about farming, animals, and the island. To the children's delight, he explained to them the significance of bird watching. He shared how watching the ducks and hunting patterns of birds, one could discern the path and speed of a current or the changing wind patterns. He taught them how to fish, hunt and swim. He showed them how to live off the land by knowing which plants and roots were edible and which to avoid. He cautioned them that danger was about when the natural hum of the island ceased.

One day while schooling his two sons, James, his youngest son, noticed a parcel of floating flowers that appeared to be thirty or more feet long. "Daddy", asked James, "how them flowers float and still grow?" Thad spoke slowly. "Son...if something in nature looks off, most times that's the time to back off. I've seen those floating flowers and each time some sort of death has been nearby. YOU STAY AWAY FROM THEM FLOWERS!! I've got my suspicions but I'm not totally sure, 'cause I didn't get too close." James understood.

Summer was coming to an end but it was still quite hot and humid. Perhaps that's why Thad's beautiful teenage daughter Lillie, had decided to sneak a late-night swim in their lake. She knew that the water would be refreshing after a long day of doing chores in the heat. The lake was cool and calm and unusually quiet ...still.

After swimming a while, she noticed the floating flowers that were usually in the marsh just some fifty yards away. She decided to swim out and investigate when out of nowhere came a familiar voice. "It's getting' kinda late little girl and oughten you begettin' home?" It was Orin Bridgewater and his no count friend Danny Parsons, sons of old fallen white gentry who seemed to enjoy drinking corn mash and recounting old stories than workin' (And both ugly to boot!). Then Orin offered up an idea: "Tell you what little girl, I think me and Danny here are HOT TOO. Whatda yah say Danny boy? Why don't we get naked and swim with Miss Lilly? "Why not?" replied Danny with a wide grin. Lilly protested, "I don't need no company and you're trespassin' right about now.

I'll scream for help!" "Scream all you want, your daddy's big ole house is way over the other side of the woods. Besides, me and Danny boy here are leavin' Hilton Head for good and we dun said our good-byes. Before the night is over, all three of us will have a memory that none of us will ever forget... especially your uppity daddy!" Both men shed their clothes and Danny being the better swimmer dove in the water quickly getting in back of Lilly. Orin marched toward her frontally. She was trapped.

As she turned to size up the position of the two men, she caught a glimpse of the floating flowers right next to Danny. Unexpectedly Danny yelled sharply and disappeared under the waterline. Orin called out to him. In an uncontrollable panic, Lilly swam quickly in a lateral direction away from the flowers and scampered onto the beach. Orin waded out farther and continued to call for Danny. It was then that the floating flower bed torpedoed Orin into the shallows three or four feet from the shoreline. Then the mound of flowers arched revealing the largest alligator that had ever been seen anywhere on the island. The animal had Danny's blood streaming from its mouth!

Orin tried to scramble backwards from the monster but to no avail. The beast was on him like a huge southern colorful patchwork quilt. It laid its mammoth body on him, but did not eat him. Shaking with blinding fear, Lilly forced herself to watch.

In the moonlight she could see that the vines of exotic flora-fauna had grown totally around the beast and that some of the flowers had even budded. Blood streamed from Orin's mouth and ears from the sheer weight of the animal that was leisurely resting atop of him. Orin, in obvious shock, turned and looked pitifully at Lilly. It was then that the full truth of the moment was revealed. Two baby alligators swam in and marched onto the beach. In a brief eerie momentary silence, a deadly montage was framed in absolute stillness. Then the carnage began with the two babies ripping at their prey's extremities. Orin yelled just one last long scream that amplified itself with the wind and echoed across the lake. He had been right. No one would hear him, except Lilly, who ran toward her home faster than she had ever run before, blocking out everything but her own heartbeat that was pounding in her ears.

As daybreak unfolded, the Standborne family posted signs that the lake was temporarily closed because of a supposed water moccasin sighting. This seemed a reasonable request to all their neighbors. In truth, Thad wanted to secure as much of the lake as possible with traps and fencing to ensure the floating flowers menace would be deterred from returning. It was a successful effort because the floating flowers were never seen in the lake again.

The fate of Orin and Danny would forever be a closely held family secret. Only they knew that the floating flowers that were seen less and less in the marsh were Orin and Danny's ever moving aquatic grave camouflaged by the aquatic scenery.

A Second Chance

(a short story by m. i. williams jr.)

Brian Cavanaugh was a chosen soul... chosen to do great things. He appeared to have found favor with God. His calling seemed unlikely to some people, given his dubious start in life. Looking back at his childhood, he had severe bronchial asthma that left him weak and sickly during his early years. His mother, Candace, encouraged him as often as his successful achievements warranted, but not to the point of spoiling him. His father was rarely around after the divorce, which explained why he frequently hung out with the wrong sort of male role models.

Although he was a good student, all of his teachers agreed that Brian had the potential to be an exceptional student-if he would only use his God-given talents. Periodically, he would even ditch school to go to the beach or just hang out reading books that truly interested him. Minor infractions seemed to follow him monthly from his adventures of going to new places during school hours.

To his credit, he always admitted his guilt and accepted the consequences without whining. But his wake-up call occurred the time that he was joy riding in one of his friend's cars when the "crew" stopped and nonchalantly asked him to watch the car while they took care of "some business".

What they failed to mention was that they were going to perpetrate a home invasion robbery. It appeared that God was with him because his fingerprints were nowhere to be found in the house when they got busted and he got off. Candace was blessed to be a surgical nurse making her skills high in demand.

Candace, wanting more for her son, announced that they were going to move to Pasadena, away from the beach, and hopefully away from his negative influential friends. It was about that time that Brian found his grandmother's old forgotten bible. He remembered how she would read him the bible in the evenings when his mother was still in school finishing her training to become a nurse. He remembered how confident that his grandmother spoke to him with a smile, declaring the bible's power and righteousness. He soon began to explore it and read it for himself. He found that he couldn't put it down. The words, the stories, and most of all the promises that it declared spoke to the hollow emptiness he often felt that his life represented.

He had been Ishmael, the Prodigal Son, and Peter, all at different times...knowing the truth yet denying it, being less than God would have him to be. If God didn't lie nor make mistakes, then God did have a purpose for him.

Having felt that he had received some insight from God, Brian went to his mother and humbled himself, promising to be the son that she deserved. Although overjoyed, she challenged him to walk the talk. He agreed. The move happened and Brian was true to his word. He was focused and his grades were stellar. He became a young community leader of sorts, volunteering at their new church home, Friendship Baptist Church. It was during his work there that he found who was to be the love of his life; a young woman by the name of Tiffany Mann. They instantly clicked and everyone could see it. The time came when Brian won a full scholarship to Washington University in St. Louis, Missouri, while Tiffany was headed to San Francisco State. It made little difference. They both excelled. Though they longed to be together physically, they waited. They both knew what God required of them. Following graduation, Brian got accepted to law school. Tiffany became a certificated teacher. Upon completing her student teaching, Tiffany proposed to Brian- after all, this was the 21st century, and he eagerly accepted.

They were married in Friendship. With God's blessing, Tiffany's steady job, and Brian's part-time job, he managed to pass the bar in record time. Upon passing the bar, Tiffany threw a grand party for Brian. It was his year! Brian had come a long way. God had bestowed so many blessings on him. He had given him a second chance, but why him? The word says that: God blesses who he blesses and curses who he curses. And it was then that Tiffany made the announcement of the evening, that Brian would have to be a good lawyer to support her and their new son! Brian wept openly.

A good lawyer was an understatement. Brian was a SUPERLATIVE lawyer. If winning cases was a baseball game, he was easily a twenty-game winner with a few no hitters to boot. A great wife, a wonderful son, a supercharged career, a big house, two paid for cars, a high credit rating and money in the bank. Life was OH SO GOOD!

But the Lord giveth and the Lord taketh away. And it doth rain on the just and the unjust.

Sean Mann Cavanaugh was the spitting image of his father physically. But that's where the similarity ended. He was a friendly and pleasant child but he was... different.

At first there were the little oddities like his inability to remember names of pictures or toys. He crawled backwards and shimmied forward. His spatial awareness was off and he would often turn and directly hit nearby walls.

As responsible and concerned parents, the Cavanaughs took their child to a specialist. Since Brian was a successful barrister, they could afford to seek the best professional help available.

After a series of tests, the results were confirmed. Sean had sensory integration issues, whereupon he had no sense of midline in his body. The right side had little correlation to the left. But the worse news was that one of the tests revealed an unexplainable "irritable focus" in the left temporal side of the brain, suggesting that he would always have some sort of learning disability. The young parents were crushed but not defeated. They each asked within themselves if they individually had in any way been responsible for their child's condition. Their doctors had assured each of them that they had not. They were merely the victims of the "Law of Averages."

Brian tried to put on a brave face for Tiff, but she knew it was just that.

"God never makes a mistake", that's what everyone kept telling them and that's what Brian accepted.

No one could find more supportive or loving parents.

There wasn't any experience that Sean didn't have or enjoy like any other kid. But as he grew, even he knew he was different. Other kids caught on to games faster. He always seemed to need additional help from others. He couldn't run or catch as well as the other kids.

Then one day Sean heard the words that he would forever hold in his spirit. A younger child was asking his mother about Sean's obvious lack of skills and she replied, "Sean's a little different...he's slow. ""HE'S SLOW!"

The words kept bouncing around in his head and heart until they brought tears to his eyes. Weeks afterwards, Sean went to his father and asked him a question that broke his father's heart: "Dad, why me? Why did God pick me to be the slow one"? The question caught Brian off guard, but he had promised himself early on that he would never lie to his son.

"Sean, I don't know why God made you different, but I do know he loves you, and you know that your mother and I love you.

I asked that same question of God Sean, and God gave me the only answer that I now give to you, my son. The answer was: Why NOT you? Am I not God?"

With tears in his eyes Sean confessed to his father: "I just want to be like you, strong and perfect". "Sean, believe me, I'm not perfect," Brian replied. "To me you are, and I want to be you". He went to his father and hugged him tightly, Sean crying aloud, Brian crying inside.

That conversation would set the course for both their lives.

Brian began to search the internet nightly to learn everything about Sean's condition. He even enrolled some of his staff and friends to help him identify sites and links of interest. Tiffany said little about her husband's pursuit, but deep inside she worried about him. But she learned early on from some of her divorced and quarrelsome friends that telling your husband what he couldn't do could lead the marriage into an unhealthy area, no matter how good the intentions were. After five years of diligent searching, Brian stumbled across an article about a Brazilian brain surgeon that seemed quite promising. Dr. Emiliano de Sousa, of the Universidad de Brasil, had been doing extensive research on the frontal lobes of lower primates, specifically the limbic system.

Dr. de Sousa of course believed that once formed, the brain was unable to regenerate additional tissue, a fact accepted by all of science.

Until recently, and only with therapy, could the brain be trained to rewire new neural pathways, and only if the neoplasm part of the brain that dealt with reasoning was undamaged.

What Dr. de Sousa discovered was that with human growth hormones in the form of stimulated brain stem-cells and with donated brain cells from a parent or relative donor, new brain cells were able to be grafted in and function.

The two problem areas being one, there were no cognitive or measurable indicators to assess the effectiveness of the process with a higher primate and two, that the donor could possibly lose some mental prowess on some level. Dr. de Sousa was well aware of the moral and ethical arguments his research presented. Already animal rights activists, abortion rights groups, and the Catholic Church had weighed in negatively. Brian's head went full tilt. Could this be so? Was this the second chance that Sean needed? How far from reality was the possibility that such an experiment could happen?

Brian was on the phone with Dr. de Sousa within the week. He had been traveling in Germany lecturing to neural interns about the newest minimally invasive frontal lobe techniques and had been unavailable.

Dr. de Sousa welcomed Brian's enthusiasm but informed him that what he desired was years away because of the need for more tests, more measurable results, more money, and finally a change of attitude from his detractors and critics. He further confessed that he was afraid that because of his ground breaking theories that his very license to practice medicine might be at risk. The good news was that certain pharmaceutical concerns in the United States were interested in his work, and had hinted that perhaps arrangements could be made for him to practice medicine and do research if he could see his way to allow them to "sponsor" him. He chose not to further elucidate on the phone. They agreed to talk further in the not-too-distant future.

For the first time in a long time Brian felt some real hope for his son. As he drove home, he allowed his mind to wander about the possibilities that science, in the 'not too distant future' would be able to provide to mankind.

In the future, birth defects like Sean's would be talked about as ancient mythological lore. He couldn't wait to tell Tiffany about his conversation with Dr. de Sousa. Unfortunately, that was not to happen. In the next instant Brian was the victim of a drunk driver. The impact caused his entire life to flash before his eyes and like an old black and white TV screen from the fifties, darkness engulfed his mind, leaving him ever so briefly, a small dot of light that was slowly fading to black. In the distance of time and space he heard Tiffany's voice say "I'll pursue his dream... freeze him," followed by a silence and an indescribable peace.

Tiffany and Sean went on living. Tiffany was able to accept that God doesn't make mistakes, but Sean continued to mourn his cryogenically frozen father for the next seven years. Then, as if by some macabre prophesy, the call came. It was Dr. de Sousa. The pharmaceutical company had lobbied some influential senators that passed a law that would allow a limited number of test groups to perform brain procedures on patients such as Sean. And since he had a frozen donor, Sean would be one of the most ideal cases.

Mother and son talked and prayed, and talked some more.

Finally, they both agreed that this is what dad had wanted for Sean. Dr. de Sousa assured them that Sean would not be in any real danger. The worse that could happen is that they would see no real change, but that no further mental diminishment could occur.

Although Sean was not aware of it, the day of the surgery would be the 8th anniversary of his father's accident. Since there had been only a memorial service, and no burial, Sean always felt that his father was just asleep. Now he eagerly looked forward to receiving a part of his father. He felt that he would finally get part of his wish.

The last thing that Sean would see before the anesthesia kicked in was his mother's smiling hopeful face.

In the operating room, Dr. de Sousa was surprised and

pleased that the father's thawed brain had ample amounts of usable cells to harvest. He was confident that using a larger quantity of the father's brain could only help Sean's chances in obtaining the desired results.

The procedure lasted for ten long hours. In that time, Tiffany prayed and reminisced how strange her life had been and how strange life could be.

Although she had never confided it to anyone, she always felt that Brian was still near. It was as though the force of his will and determination to see Sean have a better life was, an ongoing mission that in the next few hours, the success of their combined desires would be determined. She felt duty bound to see it fulfilled.

In the recovery room, Tiffany watched her only son. Over the years Sean had become more like his father in appearance-that thought brought a momentary joy from the angst that she now found herself swimming in. She left her son's side and went to the hospital chapel to pray.

Slowly he opened his eyes. "WHERE AM I?"

Dr. de Sousa soothingly reassured his patient in his Brazilian baritone accent, "You are fine Sean, you rest now. We will run some tests later to see if de cell transfer was successful."

His eyes closed and heartfelt tears flowed from them. The operation had been a complete and utter failure. Why had God done this? Had he tried to thwart the will of God and this was the awful price? He could feel him within his spirit but yet, he was GONE! WHY!!?

Truly, God curses whom he curses, and blesses whom he

blesses. His ways ARE as far from man's as Heaven is from the Earth.

Brian wept even harder as he was being wheeled back to his private room. HE WAS BACK and Sean was gone! Sean had finally received his wish in full. Sean was Brian but Brian WAS Sean. But why... why had God done this? Why had he given him... a second chance?

The Curious Curse of Carol Stanton-White

(a short story by m.i. williams jr.)

She was the youngest of three children, and by far was the most exquisite. But everyone knew that the Stanton family was destined to produce handsome children. Their mother, Laura Ross, had at one time a brief career with Ebony Magazine's Fashion Faire back in the mid-sixties. Her caramel toned complexion, smooth skin and curvaceous body always made men give her a second and even a third look. But it was her beautiful eyes that helped her make a living and drove her rise to her brief claim to fame. One look into those oversized light brown agates made every man a slave!

Leslie Paul Stanton, her future husband, was no run-of-the-mill brother either. He too was easy to look at. The two had met on a photo shoot and their mutual attraction was undeniable. He was a handsome, square-jawed, 'high yella' model from Shreveport, Louisiana.

Their romance began the minute they met as if ordained

and predestined. The ease and speed of their connection was obvious.

Knowing that the road, and marriage seldom works, Leslie retired from modeling and used his natural gift of communication and great looks to land a good job at a national retail store in Laura's hometown, of Pasadena, Ca. In one short year he was a manager. Six months later, Laura joined him permanently, completed her nursing degree, and the two were joined in matrimony as husband and wife.

With two decent paying jobs, and her family as support, the two quickly started enlarging the family unit. Their first born was Lori, a beautiful girl with honey-colored skin tone and a smile just as sweet. As she grew, she became studious to a fault. She acquired a darker shade of her mother's eyes, an absolute beauty to behold. Next, came Derrick. Fair-skinned like his father, Derrick too was quite handsome and the personification of energy. He was genuinely kind and always willing to lend a helping hand. Both children made their parents proud. One girl and one boy, both handsome, and healthy; Who could ask for anything more? The family grew, matured and prospered.

Unexpectedly, Laura again announced that she was pregnant. Carol was born. She was, well...different. She was so perfect...almost too perfect.

Her hair was light brown with distinctive streaks of gold layered throughout. She had eyes of bright crystal ice-blue, which in the sunlight seemed to turn a turquoise green. Her facial features did not resemble any of those of the rest of the immediate family, nor did her skin coloring. She appeared to be White instead of African-American. Only on the tips of her fingers and toes did she display any hint of being Black. Upon seeing his youngest daughter, Leslie Paul slightly chided his beautiful wife that Carol had six weeks to "brown up" or she had some serious explaining to do. The child never did!

As Carol grew, she seemed to possess a double portion of every positive human attribute that a person could possess. She was ever so thoughtful; generous with her time and possessions. She excelled in every subject. One would think that her siblings would have resented her but they didn't. They couldn't. They loved her because she was so lovable. Her parents tried not to show favoritism, but alas they couldn't help themselves. She was their "princess". In fact, she was a princess to everyone who encountered her. She was almost...addictive. No one could stop staring at her.

Carol's life was certainly not without its challenges. Other black children who first encountered her would always ask, "Are you White?" As though she was defending herself, she would always emphatically protest that she was as "Black" as they were. But her biggest reoccurring challenge in life was to convince strangers that she was not "stuck up" or arrogant. This became increasingly difficult because as she grew, she became more and more gorgeous. Soon, her extraordinary beauty became the very bane of her existence. As a teenager, she had on numerous occasions indirectly caused some serious auto accidents due to grown men looking at her as she walked down the street, smiling at her instead of watching the road. Several wives had slapped their husbands across the face publicly to bring them back to reality, once even in church! Instead of laughing these things off, Carol took them to heart, blaming herself for the frailties of men.

Only in the presence of her family did she truly feel safe, loved, and genuinely at ease. She was wounded deeply when she often found that girlfriends had used her to attract the opposite sex for their own purposes.

Worse still were the dates that turned out to be merely a ploy to make other girls jealous or just to be seen with a "White girl."

In truth, her ever growing beauty caused her to begin a downward spiral. She began to doubt her friendships. She questioned if she had gotten any of her jobs due to her intelligence or because of her stellar looks. She wondered if people were being sincere and genuine with her or were they saying the things that would endear her to them for their own agendas.

But worst of all were the constant stares; the conversations that seemed to stop in mid-sentence when she entered a room; the groping for words by the curious or infatuated. As an adult, life only seemed to repeat the same scenarios no matter where she went. Men promising the world to her or bringing her unsolicited gifts was almost an everyday occurrence.

Her mother tried to comfort her daughter, but she understood too well the burden of having beauty. However, she also acknowledged in her heart that Carol's beauty was beyond her experience... perhaps beyond anyone's experience.

Carol felt lonely, and worse, unsure of herself. Perhaps that is why Nicky White was able to worm his way into her world.

"Slick Nick", had always been on the periphery of the Stanton family because he was a close friend of Derrick's. He got his nickname because he was always able to talk his way into and out of any circumstance. He had never been able to "talk" to Carol because she knew how Nicky really was. But now she was lonely and Nicky, like a canine predator, sensed her vulnerability and had moved in for the kill. He seduced her and made her his own... made her his wife.

Carol thought that in time she could settle him down by giving him so much love and affection that he would surely give up all his slick ways. For a few years he did, because he took pride in introducing everyone to his wife, Mrs. Carol Stanton-White. But as his friends told him how lucky he was to have Carol he began to feel that she was yesteryear's trophy. He reasoned that if he could get her, he could get other fine women as well.

The next eight years were bitter years for Carol, but none as bitter as the last year, the year that Nicky brought home a venereal disease that left her unable to bring forth life. For this she hated him and finally divorced him.

After moving back home, Carol drifted in and out of one meaningless relationship after another. One such relationship was with a co-worker by the name of Crayton Beltran. Like every man who encountered Carol, he fell hopelessly in love with her. He wooed her and pursued her but she told him that all they could ever be were friends. He managed to get her to go out on a hand full of dates, but in the end even he realized he wasn't the one. On their last date, Crayton became verbally abusive.

As she left his car, he cursed her and her beauty by claiming that she would never find nor keep a true love with anyone else if she didn't have it with him. In truth, she felt guilty for seeing Crayton for so long because he was truly just a way to pass time. She bade him goodnight and dismissed him from her presence... forever. In her mind, she already decided to put in for a transfer so that she would be rid of him.

That would prove to be unnecessary, because Crayton never made it home that night. He had purposely played chicken with an oncoming eighteen-wheeler and lost.

In her heart she knew why Crayton had died, and she secretly carried the guilt of his death within. With that event her life seemed to be spinning downward. During this same time, her sister's marriage had fallen apart; all of which necessitated that she and her children also temporarily move back into the family home.

All this added to her sense of sadness. But then the event that sent her to the brink of a breakdown was the devastatingly tragic deaths of both her beloved parents in a highway collision. She was psychologically and emotionally crushed. Her beauty, as always was intact, but the radiance in her eyes was gone. She hated life itself. She mistrusted everything, including her own judgment. She hated God, and she even told him so. She had lost all hope of ever finding happiness. Crayton's curse had come to pass. It was in that moment of tissue-like vulnerability and self-pity that she forced herself to go back...back to her old church. Back to a place of familiarity. Back to God.

In her absence the church had called a new pastor, Pastor Henry. Carol thought that he was a pretty good preacher.

His message seemed to comfort her and soothe her soul. At the end of the service, the man next to her remarked, "My brother was in rare form today!" as he started to leave. For some unknown reason, Carol asked if he knew the pastor well. He replied that when he said "My Brother" he had meant just that. The pastor was his blood brother. They both laughed. Carol instantly felt that this man was being authentic with her. Then the old fears came back. "Does he think I'm White? Why did he really speak to me?" "I'm sorry. I'm Horace Henry, Pastor Henry's older brother". She gave her name. "Well, I hope you come back and partake of some of our Sunday soul food next week, young sister. Have a good day." And he left. Carol left church feeling better, in fact feeling a lot better. Perhaps church was the ingredient that was missing from her life. Just like Pastor Henry had said, "Turn your troubles over to the Lord. If he can handle the world's problems, yours can't be too big for him; because you are in the world, just not of it." Carol did return again and again becoming more and more at home.

She settled in as a regular attendee and became an integral part of the church to the delight of all. She often found herself talking to Horace and seeking his advice.

He was easy to talk to. She found out that he was a widower and had raised two children alone for nearly ten years. His kids were now out of the house and being single he volunteered regularly at the church. Carol didn't want to believe it but she began to be attracted to him. After about a year, she finally worked up the courage to tell him about her feelings. To her dismay, initially he didn't believe her. He told her that in every fairy tale that he had ever read, the frog never got the princess, and compared to her beauty, he was more the toad variety. He told her that he was ten years from retirement and she surely would be better off with a younger man. Carol told him that she was sure that he was the one, because he didn't lust after her but just liked her for her. To this, even he had to agree. They both laughed, and then they both began to cry.

For seven years, Carol and Horace Henry were truly

happy. The sparkle had returned to Carol's eyes. Her beauty in seven years had not remotely diminished. Being previously married, Horace had learned what it took to be a great husband. Carol felt safe with Horace, like she did when she had been with her family. Indeed, he was her family. He loved her in such a way that anyone who encountered the couple held them as being the true model of a Christian marriage. The curse of Crayton Beltran seemed to have been broken.

That coming summer the Henry's decided to go south to visit some of Carol's relatives in Shreveport. They had purchased a new caddy and secretly Horace wanted to put it on the road. So off they went to the "Glorious South."

On I-20 leaving Gladewater, Texas is where the happiness of the Henry's would come to a sudden halt. Horace saw in his rear-view mirror the familiar flashing lights of the State Highway Patrol. He had seen the squad car at the last rest stop but had paid it no mind. Carol on the other hand had. She had noticed how one of the officers had seemed to stare at her in some strange way.

As they pulled around the bend, Horace announced that he would handle it and everything would be ok. Two officers approached the car from either side.

The shorter officer spoke. "Kinda showing off your new caddy, don't you think boy?" Henry replied, "Is there a problem officer? My cruise control was set at fifty-five miles per hour, so I doubt that we were speeding." Both officers exchanged angry looks at one another. The officer continued. "Well, I say I clocked you doing nearly seventy. Why you so nervous boy? You got drugs in that fancy car? Ok, now my suspicions are up. Everybody get outta the car". Carol noticed that they had pulled off onto an extremely bushy turn-off because there was virtually no shoulder road to stop the car. They were completely hidden from the main highway. They got out of the car.

The other officer caressed Carol with his eyes and Horace noticed it. The two officers ransacked the car and of course found nothing. Sensing trouble, Horace asked for his traffic ticket so they could be on their way. At this the officer found his reason to use violence. He quickly pulled his night stick from his belt and shouted, "Don't tell me what to do nigger; I don't care if you are sleepin' with a White woman!"

The blow was well practiced and accurate. Horace's blood hit the ground before he did. Carol screamed to the top of her lungs: **"I'm an African-American and I am his WIFE!"** The other white officer pleasantly replied, "That's good, I'll feel better knowin' that we raped a nigga, instead of a nigga loving White woman."

Instinctively Carol pushed past the unsuspecting officer with such force that his gun became unholstered and landed beside Horace. She reached Horace,(whose eyes momentarily rolled open, only to be slapped upon her head and spun on her back. The short officer was on her in a flash.

He threw her dress up and scratched at her panties ripping them off. Slightly dazed, Carol laid on her back. Her scratched silky thighs slightly parted in a moment that revealed her dark golden mound. The short man stood up and grinned, "I'll flip you for who goes first." The other retorted, "Go ahead, I'm gonna kill this nigga first." Those would be his last words on this earth.

As he turned, he saw Horace propped up on one elbow

holding his gun which was followed by the sound of wind passing through his skull. The bullet was a lucky bullet because after passing through the first man, it lodged into the back of the second who had just unbuckled his pants as it settled silently into his heart. Again, Horace went unconscious.

Moments later, Carol pulled herself together and managed to get her bleeding husband into the car and to the nearest hospital. The story of the attempted murder/rape made all the major news wires. Carol's skin found under the officer's fingernails and all the other evidence proved too overwhelming to refute. The settlement for the Henry's was seven figures. Needless to say, they were set for the rest of their lives but Horace would suffer with migraines from time to time for the rest of his life. Carol would occasionally have bad dreams remembering how close the two had come to death. Horace held her that much closer, trying to love her fears away. Still, her stomach would often tie into knots. Finally, when she could stand it no longer, she went to the doctor's office. About a few days later she got a call from the office.

She began to cry. Smiling into the mirror, she wondered if she now looked any different as an expectant mother. "Better late than never", she said to her belly, as she repeatedly thanked God for her miracle.

As she returned her gaze to the mirror, she noticed something else. Something was different. Just underneath her shining blond streaked hair, just at the temples, were two matching shocks of silver-gray hair. She laughed out loud. Now "the curse" was truly broken.

WHITE MEAT

(a short story by m.i. williams jr.)

What I'm about to share with you, only one other human being has any firsthand knowledge of. To date, there has only been gossip and unsubstantiated rumors about this, but I alone know the full unadulterated truth. For years I have yearned for the truth to be known. Now that I have obtained peace within, I must tell all. Since this written account will be found with my last will and testament, I pray my family and friends not think less of me and try to understand the reason why I have withheld the truth of this tale for so many years.

First, please know that I am not an evil or vindictive man, but I willingly confess to have been the master of the practical joke, or in retrospect, perhaps its' amused slave. I used to believe that the essence of humor could be found in just about any situation. My wife has often said that my humor bordered on being described as morbid if not macabre; but she ALWAYS laughed... despite her best efforts not to.

I realized that things were getting a little bit out of hand when my children started telling their friends to watch out for me when visiting our house or when my children started checking their beds before going to sleep.

For a while I controlled myself, but as my favorite time of the year approached, the insatiable need to do something totally bizarre came upon me. Then, as if ordained by the true Deity himself, I found her! I bought the one and only **Meg**!

Meg was the remote- controlled witch from the original movie "Legend", starring the then young pup star, Tom Cruise. She stood about 5' 2". She was covered with a light green pigmentation that seemed slightly iridescent. She, with her deep black concave eyes, her perfect spindle-like teeth and spidery-leather-like arms that were adorned with long boney-like fingers spiked with talons sparkling with splendor, was truly a delicious sight of fright.

She was breathtakingly perfect...and she was mine, **ALL MINE.** Though we were to be moving soon, I knew that this last Halloween was to be the most memorable ever fulfilling a prophecy that I was to later lament. It seemed that Meg had fallen on hard times and had been sold by the studio at auction to make room for other projects.

Her new owner bought her as an attraction to create foot traffic for the grand opening to his exclusive "horror only" video shop. Meg had done her job too well. Children wouldn't even leave their parents cars to drop off the tapes.

So, being a bright business fellow, the owner put Meg on the block through the local recycler newspaper. I bought her for $20.00. I later learned, to my pleasant surprise, that my swift purchase had been quite timely because a raucous band of fraternity types had shown up offering $100.00.

Driving home with Meg was a sheer delight. Every so often I would steal an approving look into the rearview mirror only to see those deep coal black eyes peering back at me. Yes, Meg would be so much fun to work on.

Being extremely mechanically inclined, I envisioned buying her an audio transmitter for her voice, a large ratty looking Afro-wig, and some type of weather worn cape. As I let my imagination wander, I further decided to place a small remote camera in her windpipe, mount her on remote control wheels, (my son's old skate board would serve that purpose), and for the final touch, a shiny Saracen sword. This I did to the letter. Working on Meg truly brought me hours of quiet satisfaction and pleasure.

The old me would have tested Meg out on my unsuspecting family, but I resisted that and told them that I wanted to give them a dry run of Meg in the basement. I turned off the light and cleared everything out of her path.

Our basement stairs had a small storage area underneath fitted with a flimsy door.

With the stage set I went upstairs and started the show. The door slowly opened with Meg slowly raising her now mobile head saying, in my **witchiest** voice, "Hello my children come and get some candy". Slowly from under the cloak came the Saracen sword. The kids squealed and quickly scampered up the stairs.

My wife suggested that perhaps the sword was a bit much. Perhaps, I thought, but mission accomplished!

My wife, in her usual manner, forgot to inform me that she

and the kids were going to grandmas to pick up dinners that were being sold by the church. This meant that I would be eating late because grandma loved to talk. Also, as usual, she forgot to pick up extra money, which I then supplied, and they finally left me to my new pleasure- Meg.

I finally got the camera angle just right such that I was able to capture the entire room on the monitor. I then left Meg in the corner cloaked in the dark shadows where she belonged. Halloween night was going to be glorious. Though fun, working with Meg had tired me out. Being late afternoon, I decided to nap for about an hour or until my family returned with my supper. Finding instantaneous deep sleep was no problem.

How long I slept remains a mystery even now.

To this day I don't know what awakened me. A strange sixth sense filled me with what I can only describe as an anxiety attack of foreboding fear. Intuitively, I didn't yell out. I slipped from my bed and crept downstairs. Nothing! Then I heard it. Movement in the basement, the window had creaked! I instantly looked for a weapon. Nothing! Damn! Everything useful had been packed away in anticipation of the move.

Then it came to me. I tipped-toed over to the monitor and turned it on. There, passing past the moonlit window, was a moving figure. A burglar, in my house! True, I was on the verge of selling it, but it was technically **STILL MINE**. I silently thanked God that my family had gone. Next came an idea that I felt was God inspired, a revelation of such uniqueness that it bordered on genius.

I was going to scare this butthole of a burglar to death! Meg would have her first true trial run. Quietly and firmly, I took the remote control in my hand and simultaneously locked the basement door. Then I yelled to Meg through the basement door: "KILL HIM MEG! EAT HIS HEART OUT!!!" Then slowly wheeled Meg out.

Seeing through the camera lens that this fellow was Caucasian, I shrieked through Meg: "Whiiiiite Meeeeat!!" Silence. Then, again an octave higher: "Whiiiiite Meeeeeeat!!!" Again, through the door, I yelled to Meg, urging her on, "EAT HIM MEG, EAT HIM NOW!!!" Looking through the camera, I saw what can only be described as heart-stopping terror in this man's eyes. His face changing and contorting faster than 70's Disco ball hit by a strobe light.

His mouth was open as wide as any human being that I have ever seen and yet there was no sound. "Whiiiiiite Meeeeat!!" Again, deafening silence. Finally, the sound came. Something that was primeval: "AAAAAAAAAAAAAAAAAH-HHH!!!!" **GOTCHA!** Still the thief hadn't moved. So, I had Meg raise the sword ever so slowly, hoping that he would take the hint and leave out the window that he had obviously come through. He still didn't move. I swung the sword, expecting that he would finally move. He didn't. The sword passed by him, neatly taking off his shirt, leaving him standing there in his ribbed undershirt.

It was then that the intruder looked toward the darkened ceiling and cried ever so faintly: "Sweet Jesus, save me!", and he collapsed to the cement floor with a bone jarring thud, much like a freshly logged tree.

Meg and I stood silently and lost for what seemed like an eternity. Then came the worries. "What if this guy gets up and kills me? What if he dies? Can his family sue me? What do I do now?"

I decided that I would tie him up and call the police. After all HE was the criminal here, not ME! I quickly unlocked the basement door and turned on the dinky hanging bulb. I decided to tie his hands behind his back with my belt, and his feet with his own belt, if he had one. I bolted down the stairs. He had a belt, GREAT! Meg was in the way so I rolled her back into the shadows. I turned him over and quickly tied his feet. This guy was wearing $400 Italian shoes and his belt was really nice too! Who says crime doesn't pay?

Then the unthinkable happened. He moaned! He was coming to! I was in danger! I thought, "What should I do?" Once again providence spoke to me. STICK TO THE ORIGINAL PLAN! Scare this bastard into leaving! I ran over to Meg and put on the ratty Afro-wig and put the cloak around me concealing my clothes. He moaned some more.

Time was running out. I grabbed the sword. I ran back to him and fumbled so more with his belt.

I got one hand in the makeshift noose when he opened his eyes. I panicked. Then I did something that I imagine only a perverted sociopath would have done. I yanked down his pants, boxer shorts and all, and firmly grabbed his testicles with my left hand and brandished the sword in my right, and screeched "Whiiiiiite Meeeeat!" "YEEEEESSS, YEEEEEEEESSS,YES!! Whiiiiiite Meeeeat" The intruder lost all control. From beneath my wigged face, I could see every artery and vein in this poor man's face. Yanking his manhood out of my grasp, the deflated appendage began to involuntarily discharge itself.

Luckily, I was out of range. Then began this inhumanly long and cacophonous ear-piercing scream: "NOOOOOOOOOOO!!!!" The intruder then began hopping up the basement stairs, still holding the perfect pitch to his scream and also holding his manhood, belt, drooping boxers and pants, all in stride.

Upon reaching the top of the stairs, he tried to pull up his pants, only to bash his head on the doorknob. Instinctively, my humanity called out to me and I started toward the poor man to help him. I forgot that I was still wearing the wig and clutching the sword. I kindly touched his shoulder. He yelled as if he had been stabbed. Somehow, he fought off unconsciousness and managed to slam the basement door in my face.

I snatched Meg's getup off and went to resume my aid to the man. But to my utter astonishment, he was two blocks down the street before I reached my front porch, still holding the scream and his manhood firmly in place in an indescribable hopping/running manner.

As if on cue, my neighbors began to poke their heads out of their homes, each looking for answers in the face of the next neighbor. "What was all that racket? "What's going on?" "It looked like some guy was running half-butt naked down the street!!" You see anything?" Not knowing why, I said as earnestly as I could, "No, I was taking a nap". I shrugged my shoulders, smiled a false neighborly smile and slowly closed my door.

Shortly thereafter, my family returned. I had decided to speak of the night's events later on in private with my wife. Truth be told, I was wound up tighter than a clock.

Upon entering the kitchen, my wife automatically placed my supper in the microwave and gave me her ceremonious kiss on the cheek. She stopped and asked whether I was feeling alright. I quickly lied and assured her that I was fine.

Then in her routine casual manner she said, "Oh, I forgot to tell you to watch out for the assigned real estate man.

He was to come by to check and see if the repairman had fixed the leaky pipes in the basement. I told him that either you or I would be home. He said that he might be able to see it from the outside window if there was enough light." Without waiting for my response, she left the room. Suddenly my legs felt like softened play dough. I had physically and mentally tortured a poor, innocent, overzealous real estate man!

From that night on I lost all my desire to play practical jokes. About two days later I learned that the sale of my house had been completed by another associate of Mr. Hollingsworth, our real estate agent. I was informed that Hollingsworth believed that the original agent had gone to the wrong house in the neighborhood and had encountered something so bizarre that he would have to spend several months in a sanitarium located out of state.

I later learned that upon his release that he left the country and joined some sedate, vegetarian, community orientated order of Franciscan monks that devoted their lives to assisting mankind and the understanding and acceptance of cultural differences.

As for Meg, having lost my need to scare anyone, I passed her on in her original form to the very raucous fraternity that had initially desired her, making a modest profit of $80.00.

With this written account of what happened that fateful pre-Halloween night those many years ago, I close a regrettable chapter in my life that even now seeks that poor man's forgiveness and your understanding.

Another Sunny Southern California Day

(a short story by m.i. williams jr.)

The day began as just another sunny Southern California day. But this day would be a defining moment in my life. It was a day that most Southern Californians would forever remember with awe and terror. For that was the day of the "Big One". It happened on December 21, 2028 at seven thirty-five in the morning. It was the day that the California sun and all the planets in the solar system aligned causing the greatest gravitational shift on the earth's axis ever recorded, and an earthquake rising to 9.98 on the Richter scale. The devastation was incomprehensible.

Liquefied earth in Malibu mercilessly swallowed homes as if they never were. Incessant coastal waves of 40 and 50 feet, shot yachts across the ocean like dice, landing them upside down like toy boats in a giant bathtub. I had seen all these sights from the Pacific Coast Highway, and had lived to talk about it. Commuters less than 100 yards from me weren't so lucky. Some of the unearthed boulders on the hillsides of scenic

Pacific Coast Highway had, in many cases, meted out indiscriminate injuries and crushing death.

As I look back on that day, the earthquake would prove to be the most rational and the most believable part of my day.

As a sales rep, I made it my job to know the freeways and connecting routes in and around the city of Los Angeles. The pharmaceutical company that I worked for allowed me to use their minivan as my own vehicle, complete with a cell phone. I called my wife's cell to see if my family was okay. They were well but understandably frightened. My only problem was getting to them. The devastation was reminiscent of a war zone.

Gasoline fumes and small vehicular fires dotted the Pacific Coast Highway. People in shock and disbelief roamed aimlessly along the road or sat blankly staring into the distant raging ocean that from time to time, reached the main highway. According to the copter reports, no road was undamaged for more than a five-mile stretch. I drove to an emergency center, only to be asked to leave since I wasn't hurt or in need of any type of emergency assistance. I really didn't mind. For being cooperative, I was given an army ration of food. I gave them some free samples of a new antibiotic drug and wide surgical gauzes.

As I was leaving the center a California National guardsman noticed my packed tent that I had used the previous weekend in the back of my van. He suggested that camping out might be to my advantage for at least one night. Great idea I thought.

I was a decent outdoorsman and I enjoyed it. Being a dutiful husband, I called my wife and told her of my decision. She concurred and gave me her usual "be careful speech" about wild bikers, and of course, wild women. I Googled out the surroundings and decided on an area in the Santa Monica recreational area that seemed easily accessible. As I drove along the ever-narrowing path to the camping area, I could still hear the faint sirens and helicopters that managed to intrude upon this quiet place of nature. There was no evidence that the quake had even so much as broken a tree limb or disturbed a rock. And yet, something was different. No birds. No squirrels. No trees rustling...no sounds. Complete stillness. There was an unsettling eeriness about it and yet the scenery was so beautiful. I drove on taking in the serenity of the hills. Then, without warning, as is the pattern of all earthquakes, an aftershock occurred. But this aftershock was different.

It was followed by a cacophonous blast of rushing swirling wind. My van rattled in its wake. I stopped and checked the map. I couldn't quite figure out where I was. I cautiously drove on. Suddenly, from nowhere, a fence barred my path. I thought that I had missed my turn. I got out stretching my legs when I saw through the trees, a curious sight. There between a sentinel of trees was a body of water. I went back to the van to look at the Google map. Funny, I thought, that lake isn't on here. Yet there it was. Curious. I strained to see from atop the fence. The water appeared choppy. No doubt the wind had spanked it too on its way east. In an instant I decided that an evening of fishing and camping by a lake would be a treat after such an unsettling day. I squeezed the chain from around the post with my tire iron, drove in, replaced the chain loosely around the post and pointed the van down the path toward the lake.

I was deceived by the distance to the lake. After more than a mile the path disappeared and I found myself maneuvering between various species of trees until there was little room to even turn around. At that point, I parked the van.

I was thankful for my wife's continued encouragement to prepare an earthquake bag that held my Pocket Fisherman, fishing knife, sealed drinking water, solar blanket, soap, hard candy, old tennis shoes and a change of clothes. I quickly changed into the clothes, grabbed the tent and related gear and locked the van. Evening was advancing quickly and I wanted to be pitched and ready by nightfall. The lake was just beyond the ridge. I could smell it. It reminded me of the ocean. The ground felt surprisingly hard for a lake area.

As I topped the ridge, the magnitude of the lake was humbling. There seemed not to be any beach per se, only one huge finger of land jetting out into the water like a bridge, 12 yards wide and approximately 20 yards in length, and standing some 10 feet above the water line. The water was now like glass. In some childish way at that moment, that lake seemed to be my personal possession to enjoy and commune with as I saw fit. Since the topography left me little choice, I headed toward the peninsula to pitch my tent and set up camp. Looking at the underlying rim of the finger of land I deduced that the high-water mark wouldn't be anywhere near the surface. I was sure that I wouldn't wake up swimming in my tent.

A lone pine tree stood proudly at the mouth of the land mass. A stack of boulders and tree roots made a convenient bridge to the main part of the camp site. Within 30 minutes the tent was up. I choose to pitch near the edge so that I could enjoy the small waves lapping against the walls of the land's end. Securing the tent was a must since I had already experienced one freakish wind. The ground was so unbelievably hard, yet wild grass was abundant and soft. It reminded me of the grass found on the face of mountains and hills that wild cattle and sheep grazed on.

As I once again peered over the lake, this time I noticed two small tops of trees close to the shore, as if they were growing diagonally out of the wall of the shore line. "How odd", I thought. "There's no end to Nature's wonder". I picked my way back across the boulder bridge to get fire wood and dug for worms. Securing both, I proceeded to cast my dandy Pocket Fishermen in the lake and built a fire worthy of my old Cub Scout training. Night was now conquering day with ease. I was pleased with my camping efforts and yet a profound sadness crept upon me that I had been trying not to acknowledge all day...the human misery that lay outside this peaceful place.

The poor people of Los Angeles, many of whom were now homeless, tired, scared, injured, full of anxiety and in some cases were mourning their dead. I felt in some way guilty, for my losses were minimal and yet I also felt a great sense of relief. At that moment, my pocket fisherman alerted me to a catch. With no net, I knew this fish would be hard to reel in. Just then the fish broke the plane of the water. A ten pound something, probably a trout. We struggled for about ten minutes. It was dark now, and I was having the time of my life. Then I got an idea. Reel him in and flip him against the hard rim. I only needed to take some of the fight out of him. I reeled evenly and at the crucial moment jerked the line and smacked him into the wall. It worked. I then dragged him close to the bridge where in an instant some water was sprayed over me. Where had that come from? No matter. There would be fish with my army rations tonight! Fresh fish over an outdoor spit was good eatin'.

As I ate, I thought how the fish tasted more like Pacific Ocean Rock Cod than a fresh water fish.

Indeed, a little of the water that had sprayed into my mouth was more reminiscent of the ocean than a fresh water stream. Probably the soil make-up... what the hell did I know.

The night was extremely warm and pleasant, and the moon was bright and full. I had been reading and watching some birds swim by when out of the corner of my sagging eyelids I thought I saw one slip under the waterline as if he had been snagged. Instantly, the flock took flight. "Crazy birds", I thought. I arose and went into the tent. Suddenly, the tent shook as if by someone's hand. I darted out to investigate. There was nothing. Another aftershock? Sure. Of course. But the tent was dripping water. A wave? No! There wasn't any discernible tide. I steadied myself. The air was still. I could only hear the beating of my heart. An animal of some sort? I retrieved my pen flashlight. Nothing. Ten minutes. Nothing. I relaxed.

Again, water splashed loudly. I bolted out of the tent, only to see large ripples bouncing outwardly about 10 yards from the peninsula point. I laughed. It must be a big fish. It gave me a whole new meaning to the phrase: Fish are jumping!!! I laughed out loud until my laughter echoed as if resounding off a canyon wall.

I decided to read some more of my boring book that I had been reading all week, **Crisis Management**. I threw a few more logs on the fire and watched the sparks and ash dance and disappear over the lake. I stared into the water and looked at the reflection of the moon. I peered harder. There seemed to be two moons in the water. Yellow reflections seemed to be coming up from the depth of the water. Closer and closer, illuminating like cats' eyes in the water! Coming, coming up like the headlights of a bus, toward the surface, toward the land, toward me! I stood there paralyzed, transfixed in the moment.

What I saw next, my mind could not grasp. I saw, thought, and moved in slow motion. My knees shook out of control and gave way to my terror. There, before my eyes, was a fish the size of my van totally extended out of the water, 30 yards from my face. The wind of its wake caused me to roll onto my back. The resulting reentry splash sent water hurling in all directions and left my once proud fire gasping only with steam and mud.

Still unable to process the magnitude of the last 20 seconds I slowly stood.

There at the foot of the peninsula, its massive head looking up at me, the fish waited, somehow knowing that I would come to reconfirm what my senses had previously relayed to me. Its head was contoured like a Moray eel but its mouth was shaped like an Archer fish. The blackened water hid the greater part of its body but the tail was dolphin or whale-like, enabling it to float stationary.

Then, without a warning, the life struggle began with a massive shot of water to my chest that lifted me off my feet and propelled me backward barely missing the dying fire. I was partially dazed from my backward landing. I was quickly brought to by another gush of water, this time from the side. This thing was trying to knock me off this small finger of land. I quickly surmised that it was quick and accurate. **Crisis management: Lesson number One. Size up the situation. What are you up against? Why is it a Crisis?** Answer: This thing is some kind of 'throwback'!! It eats birds. Ergo, He'll Eat Me Too! **Crisis management:**

Lesson number Two: What is the worst-case scenario? What do you absolutely not want to happen? Answer: I do not want to be eaten!

Crisis management: Lesson number Three: What are your options? Answer: Stay low to the ground and crawl to the tent to get my knife and at the same time use the tent as a buffer between me and the fish. My main goal was simple. Get the devil off this peninsula in one piece!!

Maintaining my psychological equilibrium against being stalked by a fish demanded all the inner control that I could call forth. I could taste the panic in the form of bile in my throat. "Damn", I thought, "my phone was in the van and I was miles from help and I was alone." Worse still, I was crawling on the ground hiding from a fish! As scared and humiliated as I was, I continued to crawl toward the tent. I felt its presence, waiting, stalking. I was almost there when a gush of water whizzed over my head. I stopped. Then unable to control myself, I darted into the tent. Instantly blasts of water tore at the 10 x 10 blue dome. Quickly, I grabbed the fishing knife and slid it in my waistband.

I decided to time my escape in between the water blasts and seek refuge behind the tree (or in it) until I could maneuver over the bridge to the hillside. I waited. Nothing. Two minutes went by. Nothing. The fish won the waiting game. I couldn't stand not knowing what it was doing. I scampered out of the dome. I had done so just in time. For in the next instance, what I saw defied the laws of gravity. I saw the fish soaring over my head, diving headlong into the tent, knocking it from its moorings, ripping it from the peninsula pushing it and itself over the side carrying it into the depths of the lake.

I stood and watched with disbelief as my bright blue tent deflated and abruptly disappeared with only a residue of expelled air bubbles to mark it watery descent. Again, its yellow eyes of death broke the surface of the water. I couldn't move, I couldn't think. It was then that the entire truth unfolded.

As I watched my nemesis swim in circles 30 yards southeast of me, I had allowed my flank to be unguarded. The water hit my back with a tremendous force and a sting so violent, that it felt like fire. My body rolled off the table top land mass like a spider hit by a gust of wind.

God must have been watching, for I found that my left arm was wrapped around a horizontal tree root that was just below the plane of the surface. That was the good news. The bad news was my arm was broken.

Somehow, I managed not to pass out and slip into the water. I traded arms with the root and began the struggle to make it to the top before one of the two fish either shot me with their water cannon or just plain knocked me off the root. Groping under the dark ledge, I managed to find footing and then some leverage. I fought off blacking out more than once. Then, as I made my final approach, the fish made one of its only two errors. As I grasped for the surface, I knew I had but one chance to get it right. I was too weak for a second chance. I swung my leg over the edge pinning my broken arm underneath me, screaming in pain. It was then that one of the fish hit me squarely in my butt with enough water pressure to push me onto the surface. I proceeded to pass out relatively safe from the fish's shot due to the awkward angle of my body position.

As I lay there, my mind began to try to make sense of what

was happening. This was no lake! This WAS Ocean Water!! Trees

don't grow diagonally out of lakes, but they do on hillsides.

The soil was hard because this was an old mountainside. But how did the ocean get up here? Simple. Many mountain ranges near the coast sit on water caves and water crusts. Huge earthquakes, earth fissures, add one freak tsunami, and voila, one instant mountainside ocean lake. But where did these throw backs come from? Surely, they were some deep 'earthquake-marine gumbo' stirred from the very bottom of the ocean, pre-historic...from parts unknown." I momentarily blacked out again.

A gentle wisp of cool air brought me back to consciousness simultaneously reviving the dull ache in my swollen broken arm. **Crisis management: Lesson number Four. Get into action- NOW!** I was going to crawl over to the tree come hell or high water.

While pulling my knees around, I swung my disabled limb skyward and proceeded to crawl toward the tree. Twenty yards now looked like 2 miles. As if on cue, the two fish took turns battering me on each side with uncanny accuracy. I surmised that they had backed up and adjusted for the angle and windage. Fortunately for me, it made the water force less punishing. Fifteen more yards. The water stopped. I crawled faster. Ten more yards. Still no water! I was going to make it!

I propped myself against the base of the tree, resting my throbbing legs in the boulders. During the struggle, I hadn't thought of the time. My scratched watch revealed it to be 9:47 p.m. I wondered if I would ever see a new day. I looked across to the rocky bridge. Escape was just a few desperate yards away. Suddenly, I realized what the fish were waiting for. While crossing the bridge I would be TOTALLY exposed! One good barrage of water and I would be in the lake, ocean, ocean/lake. I needed to test my theory. I picked up a large rock and hurled it as far as I could against the bridge causing a moderate echo. The two massive heads broke the water line with a symmetry and guile that sent a shudder through my entire body. Not seeing me, they instantly disappeared below the surface.

I decided that only stealth would be feasible as a strategy for escape. I needed to maneuver the bridge in total silence through the darkness. I summoned all my resolve and what little courage I had left. I closed my eyes and said a prayer. Then I had a last-minute idea. I picked up two good size stones, turned around quickly and hurled them 45 degrees apart into the different water sides of the peninsula.

As if on cue, the fish went to investigate. I began to swiftly but quietly transverse the jagged bridge. Three-quarters of the way, I stumbled on the bridge, landing on my broken arm. I fought back the scream. I got up and within 5 yards I heard the now familiar sounds of water whizzing about my head. Then, as if a sixth sense called to my inner most sense of self-preservation, within two feet of the end of the bridge, I dove for the abbreviated shore line.

I rolled upon some leaves and underbrush just in time to witness one of the fish throwing itself onto the bridge and shore, flailing its tubular mouth within three yards of me trying to knock me back into the water. That was the second mistake. I lost all my composure. Blind rage was all that I felt. I forgot about my fear, my safety, and my painful arm. I saw this thing as a spoiled, vicious, ravenous dog. Lower than a dog, a stupid mindless fish that needed to be taught a lesson. Without thinking I reached for my fishing knife still lodged in my waistband. I stood erect and ran over to the beast. Time again slowed down. The beast froze. It knew what was coming. Screaming and running toward it, my knife found its mark in the bull's eye of its black pupil ringed with bright fluorescent yellow.

The beast stiffened. Neither of us moved. Then the sound of agony; a thousand fingernails being scratched over a chalkboard at 1000 decibels. The sound propelled me backward to the safety of the ledge-like shoreline wall. I looked down at my hand. It was covered with a pus-like substance that was cold and smelled like rancid sardines. In what seemed to be in one motion, the beast jerked on to its other side and dove back into the water. I don't know where I found the will or the strength, but I climbed the hill to the ridge. Upon making it over the ridge, I again fell unconscious.

In the wee hours of the morning, I was sure that I felt another strong aftershock, but my body ignored it. As morning arrived, I sat up, hoping that the previous night's drama had all been a bad dream brought on by a bad case of food poisoning. My arm reassured me that it had been quite real. **Crisis management: Lesson number FIVE- Assessment and reevaluation of your efforts**. Answer: I was alive. I don't know what made me turn around to look at the lake for a last time. I just knew I had to. As I turned, the reality of what I saw sent a new shock of horror throughout my body. As I pondered the scene of the struggle, I peered into a massive canyon.

A canyon that was at least two football fields straight down.

Gone was the water. Gone was the peninsula. Standing there was the same body of land but without water it was a magnificent cliff with drooping trees jetting diagonally underneath it. I shuffled a few feet closer to peer over the ridge. There on the opposite wall, looking like the dot on the end of a sentence made up of trees was my blue mangled tent. Walking away, and speaking aloud, I declare in a voice of finalization "Unbelievable!" Nature, defying my pronouncement, rattled the earth once more with an aftershock that was barely discernable. Mockingly, I laughed out loud. My laughter halted abruptly when the cliff, the former peninsula where I previously stood, crumbled and fell away, taking both of the diagonal trees with it over the curved canyon wall.

Crisis management: Lesson number Six-Determining the conclusion to the crisis.

The van was just where I had left it. My keys had remained in my pocket the entire time. Wearily, I drove back to the path and safely through the fence. As I replayed my saga, I asked myself who would believe me? and WHY? No answers came.

I could hear it now: "Did you hear the one about the giant water cannon fish that some black guy saw in the mountains." No. No thanks. I decided to tell everyone that the earthquake got me. They would nod a sympathetic nod and welcome me back into the fold. But I knew. I would always know. The proof was that I was alive. As I drove on the road, I witnessed the sun breaking through the clouds, ready to do its daily duty of imparting light... giving us yet another sunny Southern California day.

The Reef

(a short story by m.i. williams jr.)

Adrian lived a life that most children enjoyed only through adventure and fantasy books. His was a life surrounded in a love and comfort that one could almost feel. His island home was continually being caressed and washed by sweet clean fresh air and tanned by a mild sun that seemed to grow everything on the island faster, larger and healthier than anywhere else.

Every day he fished, canoed or swam in the warm ocean. The ocean felt as though it was part of the family because every good and memorable time seemed to include it. But the most wonderful and defining thing about his island home was the reddish castle-like reef that appeared to protect his home and all its' inhabitants.

People on the island claimed that most of them received their dark reddish hue from the reef itself. Adrian loved his home, and yet he longed to see more of the world; especially the mainland. Nothing dramatic or unusual ever seemed to happen on his island home, every day the same... paradise.

Adrian, like the other children, received a proper education.

Indeed, his parents were leaders on the island and one day he would be expected to take his father's place on the council on the big island. But a boy of ten got bored just thinking of those grown-up type of things.

One perfect day, Adrian was sitting on the beach enjoying the majestic view of the ebb and flow of the blue water tide. In a moment of curiosity, he decided to test his aim by throwing some of the smooth sand scrubbed multicolored rocks at the jagged edge of the reef. After several tries, the boy hit the tip of the reef chipping off a small edge. As he turned to leave, a large unexpected wave arose and swept the shore, drenching and driving him face down into the sand.

Scrambling to his feet, he looked down and saw what appeared to be the same rock that he had thrown and a second reddish chard that appeared to be part of the reef. As he turned to leave, he thought he heard a mocking voice say, "Ha". He turned about to see who had mocked him but to his surprise, not a soul was in sight. Discerning no one, he became frightened, and swiftly ran home.

Feeling a sense of cowardice, Adrian was reluctant to tell his "Grand'Mere" about his strange experience.

But as usual, he didn't have to because Grand'Mere with her island wisdom, knew something was amiss with her only grandchild. "Adrian, what is it that you wish to ask Grand'Mere?" Adrian could never hide anything from her, but he started slowly. "Grand'Mere, what is so special about the reef?" A knowing smile graced Grand 'Mere's face and she retorted: "Why is that old reef of interest to you? Did something unusual occur today?" "Well, I'm...I'm not sure", Adrian replied hesitantly.

He then proceeded to tell the day's event to his Grand'Mere while she listened quietly as she always did. When he had finished, Grand'Mere patted her hand on the chair that had belonged to Grand'Pere and Adrian sat next to her.

Now, it was Grand'Mere who started slowly. "There are things in life that just **ARE** Adrian. They cannot be explained, only understood. What I am about to tell you, only a handful of people know because there are only a handful of us who are still alive who remember any part of the early history of our island.

My father, your great-grandfather, was the last chief of the island before we went to the council system. Way before his time, the reef had always been there. Our people would fish in front of the reef and once a year we would give the reef and the ocean a tribute of our crops and place them on the reef itself.

We would do this early in the morning in the first month of the two moons. By the next morning the crops would be completely gone, but the reef always appeared to be nearly twice as high until the next full moon. All during the year the fishing was plentiful as were our crops. During the rough storm season, the reef appeared to become thick and jagged which kept out the high waters and man-eating fish like the spotted whale and the white sharks. I remember my father telling my mother that I would always be protected in the shadow of the reef. Indeed, no child has ever been harmed while in the confines of the reef."

Grand'Mere now looked directly at Adrian. "When I was about four years old, a tall ship came bearing men with pale faces. I had never seen a white man before and I was frightened. My father told me that the men rowed a small boat through the reef and brought gifts to us, trinkets and cotton materials that were foreign to us.

At first, we welcomed these strangers who spoke in a strange tongue. But as time went on, they became abusive, so much so that my father, as chief, asked that they should leave. The men did leave, or so we thought. They returned the next day in their small boat with their big guns!

My father said that he had been forewarned of something bad by the spirits as he was walking on the beach that night in front of the reef... as if he were having a waking dream. So, when the white men herded the leaders of the village to the beach in front of the reef with their big guns, my father was not surprised. Indeed, he had foreseen this.

My father said that their leader said something like this: "We have guns and in truth you are a bunch of savages. We are claiming this entire area for the King of France, and now and forever YOU WILL BE HIS LOYAL SUBJECTS!

We will teach you our laws and our ways and in time you will learn obedience and thereby become happy, civilized and content. But for now, a show of your acceptance will be that you kneel before us and swear your loyalty to the king and to the new social order."

Among the white men were two holy men who, according to my father, complained that what they were doing was not right. Angered by their dissent, the leader ordered them to stand to the side or be placed in the ship's brig. So, they stood aside from the main group. I was not there but I was told that my father turned to the other leaders, held up his hand, and motioned for them to bow backwards.

As they bowed, my father dropped his sarong revealing his bare behind to the invaders. Then all the leaders began to laugh loudly to the surprise of the white men. Your great-grandfather's bare behind would be the last thing that most of the invaders would ever see. For in the next instant the air over the beach was filled with long arrows and spears that rained down death on the invaders from behind the trees that lined the beach. My father said that the men fell to the ground with a quickness like rotten coconuts falling from a tree. Then something strange happened. A few of the wounded men managed to reach their small boat and starting rowing towards the direction of the tall ship.

As they approached the reef it began to quickly grow spear-like tips from out of the water. The men tried to dodge them but there were too many. Finally, I was told, two of the spear tips ripped the small boat into several pieces. As they swam for their ship, their bodies were stabbed repeatedly by the reef. Then my father said he and the entire village witnessed something that defied all explanation.

The entire reef arose out of the ocean like a tsunami wave, straight up, and impaled the tall mountain-like ship.

The cries from the men left on board could be heard only momentarily because the spotted whales and white sharks awaited them anxiously and mercilessly devoured them. Only the two white holy men on the beach were left alive.

The next day my father and my mother took me down to the reef with the entire village to give a special offering. As was our custom, we brought our crops and personal offerings. I remember on that day that after the last offering was given a huge but gentle wave came upon the beach. It was waist high and my father quickly picked me up as did the fathers of the other children. When the wave receded, there was a huge mound of fish that no man could count. The village gathered up all of the fish and celebrated the protection from the reef with a magnificent feast.

In time the holy men taught us that God had used the reef to bring forth a miracle. We eventually learned their language and became Christians. And the holy men stayed and mixed their blood line with ours." It was at that point that Adrian blurted out: "Is that why Sean and Marie are lighter than most of us?"

Grand'Mere smiled and merely nodded her head once in affirmation. They indeed were descendants of the two holy men. Adrian was now overwhelmed with excitement, followed by concern. "Grand'Mere, does the reef still protect us? Does it still have powers?" "One cannot say grandson, but still, no child has ever been harmed while he or she is within its walls. Although we no longer give the reef tribute, we still protect it from the outside world by not allowing pollution, or any type of destruction to enter its area. The reef is a part of us." With that, Adrian hugged his Grand'Mere and thanked her for sharing the history of their island and the reef.

Early the next morning, Adrian went to the beach... to the reef. In a loud voice he cried, "I am sorry for disrespecting you. Please forgive me! I have brought you an offering of flowers and sliced fruit from my own little garden. Please accept them as a sign of my gratitude and sorrow."

He then waded out and gently shoved the small boat-like basket toward the reef. He watched it for about twenty minutes until it seemed to suddenly sink beneath a single slapping wave. As he walked toward the beach, he turned once more to look at the reef with reverence and deep reflection. It seemed to take on a deep red color, redder than he had ever seen it before.

A thought came to him. One day he would become part of the Council. He had to. How else would he be able to protect his island paradise, his home? Then without warning, a large warm gentle wave came ashore about waist high to Adrian. When it receded, there before his feet, were two of the largest halibut fish that he had ever seen in his life. Adrian smiled and bowed humbly to the reef. He quickly picked the fish up, and hurried joyously home.

The following story is a fictional account of the writer's imagination, written in 2012 and copyrighted in 2014. Any similarities or coincidental information is in no way related to the Los Angeles fires of January 2025. Thank You

Transformation

(a short story by m.i. williams jr.)

Altadena, Ca has always been my town and I know it well. Its claim to fame back in the day was that it was the home of the Hollywood comedy icons, the Marx Brothers, and at one time it was a serious contender for the title of top fresh citrus producer in the sunshine state.

As usual, the housing developers gained the upper hand and transformed the city into a quiet uneventful bedroom community nestled against the San Gabriel Mountains. To its credit, rows of fruit trees are still hidden in resident's backyards and continue to produce sweet juicy fruit that feed the residents and the native wildlife.

As with many mountain communities, Altadena has endured many fierce and destructive wildfires that fortunately have never destroyed any homes, but quite often burned away much of its beautiful trees and animal habitats. The only silver-lining to these fires was that the soil was thoroughly enriched with nutrients.

It seems that no foot of land is not without some sort of vegetation or flora- fauna.

I often felt that my gardener and I were in a never-ending battle against the ever-present growing weeds and hedge vines that literally seemed to grow overnight. Yet, I too was a beneficiary of the most recent mountain fires. This year not only did the ash nourish the soil around my orange trees to produce a bumper crop of sweet navel oranges, but the residual ash also fell on my house and qualified me for a federal funds clean-up program.

Said ash handed me a substantial profit. I love Altadena! It would be months later that I would learn the real truth that precipitated my inclusion in the "ash abatement" fund. It seems that years ago the Jet Propulsion Laboratory (JPL) had contaminated Altadena's underground water supply with arsenic, a dash of radioactive material and some never yet explained bio-plastic materials.

The cleanup cost was astronomical, taking a big bite out of JPL's budget. Since JPL was located near the epicenter of the fires, it too was able to apply for and received substantial federal monies that appeared to be equal to their original clean-up outlay. It is in the context of the cleanup of my home that my story begins.

After cutting away a small mountain of dead vines and raking the leaves into a pile, I spotted what I thought was an old rug. Upon closer inspection I saw that it was an animal carcass. To my surprise it was that of a medium sized dog. I wondered how he died, and how he had come to be in my backyard. Cautiously turning it over with my rake, a stream of silverfish, ants and roaches scampered into the underbrush followed closely by what can only be described as a rather larger pack of reddish wolf spiders that seemed to be superfast and efficient in snapping up all the little grubs. These guys were master hunters. "God how I hate spiders," I recalled saying. And I knew why. As a toddler in my crib, I saw my first spider. It moved ever so slowly towards me. I was terrified. I remember screaming: "The Hand, The Hand, The Hand!!!

My grandmother came rushing to the crib and snatched me up. She killed the spider and allowed me to sleep the rest of the night with she and my grandfather. Spiders! Yuck! I decided to rake up most of the vines into several stacks and put them out for the garbage truck the next day along with the carcass. With my last swipe of the rake, I suddenly felt a need to stop.

My hair stood on end. It felt as if there was a presence near me.

I wheeled around and saw nothing. I stood there a few more moments and the feeling quickly subsided. "I must be tired," I thought, and strolled into the house.

Bright and early, I arose to beat the garbage truck. Before I tackled the dusty leaves and vines, I decided to water the lawn to beat the hot California sun. Not being able to put it off any longer, I put on my dust mask and goggles and began to stuff the leaves into the plastic cans. Again, the feeling of a presence was upon me. I froze in a state of fear with an acute awareness of my surroundings.

My eyes slowly and cautiously swept across the area, searching, looking. The silence was deafening. I could feel my heart pounding in my ears. Then, I saw what I didn't want to see. My eyes met its eyes. My brain refused to process what my eyes were telling it. It was reddish brown. It was hairy. It was the size of a small king crab. But it wasn't a crab at all. It was a spider...a wolf spider, and it was holding a dead field mouse in its fangs, jagged fangs that were stained red with blood.

My knees went weak and began to quiver. They felt like rubber bands. I could feel my entire body producing perspiration through every pore at an accelerated rate.

I willed myself to move backwards. It sensed something was about to happen and it stood up on all eight legs. It WAS as large as a king crab. Its leg tuffs were quite hairy and well developed like those of a short distance runner.

I backed up and ever so slowly picked up the water hose simultaneously putting the rack down. I turned the nozzle to full blast. I thanked God that I hadn't turned off the water. Aiming for its eyes I fired my water gun. It stood and easily absorbed the frontal attack and with blinding speed dashed to its right still carrying the mouse.

It was only then that I realized how much potential danger I had been in, because as I turned to shut the water off, I saw the second spider scampering out of the pile of leaves that I had been raking. It wasn't quite as large as the first spider, but just as creepy. I let out a girlish scream and ran into the house straight to the bathroom just in time to relieve myself.

My first call was to Animal Control. The guy listened to my story but told me that my situation was more under pest control... then he said something revealing. He gave me the phone number to a professor at Cal-Tech, one Dr. Charles Jamison.

When asked why he had done so, he replied: "Yours is not the first type of call we have received from Altadena". I made the call. After telling Dr. Jamison my tale he asked me if I still had the carcass of the dog, he wanted it. Then I became curious.

Why would a technological school like Cal-Tech be interested in a biological abnormality like these spiders? To this day I don't know why, but I blurted out: "Does this have anything to do with JPL?" After a moment of uncomfortable silence, he suggested that we meet at my house.

Within the hour Dr. Jamison and I met. Dr. Jamison chose his words carefully: "If by accident or design the genetic evolution of a species could be altered, that alteration could have profound and possibly positive results for mankind. Indeed, such an altered species DNA, if chemically synthesized, could have profound effects on mankind's ability to travel in space and investigate new worlds. Such a discovery could transform the very rules of biological science. Let me blunt my friend. The possibilities that could come from the research and development of such a unique specimen would also be worth millions of dollars. This new species, for whatever reason, has chosen your backyard as its hunting ground on two occasions.

Such a specimen alive or dead would probably propel science years ahead and make you a very rich man." But he quickly added, "Discretion is the key. A panic-stricken public does no one any good. Hysteria has been a stumbling block to scientific progress since the beginning of time." With that said he handed me an envelope that contained $5,000, hastily leaving with the carcass of the dog.

My downfall in this story was my greed. I kept repeating to myself the phrases, "worth millions of dollars" and "make you a VERY RICH man!" The next day I put my plan into action. Calling upon latent engineering skills, I set a trap of netting and canvass complete with some live hamster bait. I was putting the last slip knot in when out of my peripheral vision I saw it, the mother of all spiders. It was the size of a miniature Shetland pony. Its myriad black eyes were all focused on me.

Looking at its muscular make-up, and with no weapon, I knew I was clearly outmatched. I now knew what really happened to the medium sized dead dog. The sickening image of the dead field mouse flashed before my mind. I dove for the canvas net bringing it crashing around me.

The spider wasted no time pursuing me. I felt it land on top of the canvass over me. It quickly began to shred the cover as one would rip sheets with a knife. I moved feverishly under the netting and canvas. Nearing the end of the canvas, I was able to fling a great deal of the cover over the back of the animal and grabbed my rake.

I swung the steel tines at the cover with all my might. I drew first blood as evidenced by the bright red stain on the gray canvas. It momentarily retreated about eight feet giving me time to reach inside the shed door to get my machete. I was now feeling a little more confident. Why I'll never know, because it then rushed me head-on knocking me off my feet and into my half-folded ladder.

The blow caused me to drop the machete. Quickly I put the length of the ladder between us as a shield of protection. It snapped and thrashed at the ladder with a force and speed that had it not been for the maneuverability of the lightweight aluminum, I surely would have been the next carcass. The machete was about five feet away from my reach. I knew I had to reach it quickly or die for failing to do so. I then unfolded my end of the ladder and shoved it towards my attacker with the last of my fleeting strength.

The thrust of the ladder shoved the attacker back about six feet. It was then that I was able to grab the blade. Unexpectedly, it was able to pin the ladder to the ground and managed to land it on top of me!

We both drew blood this round. He impaled me with one fang in my side and me coming underneath through its exoskeleton straight to the skull with the machete. The damn thing came crashing back down on the ladder pushing out what little air that I had left.

I momentarily blacked out. Moving ever so slowly, with a scream I managed to extricate myself from the ladder and the thing. I went to get up but the wound in my side took me aback and I fell to my knee.

Looking at the wound I could see a mixture of blood and a watery, pus-like substance that burned. Finally standing up I was able to view the thing. The eyes had now faded to a dull purplish color. For reasons still unknown to me, instead of first caring for my wound, I had to turn it over on its back. With a rush of adrenaline and a new found strength I did. What I saw horrified me.

It was carrying a small egg sack, and there was some discernible movement in it. I thought, "What the hell could impregnate such a huge thing?

It didn't matter, because I was going to bludgeon whatever was in that sack.

Determined to be the ultimate victor I grabbed my sledge hammer from the shed, dragged it over and raised it like Thor. It was then that once again my greed kicked in:

... "worth millions", and "make you a VERY RICH MAN". I dropped the sledge and reached for my cell phone that somehow stayed located on my hip. "Funny I thought... my wound doesn't hurt as much." I rationalized that I was probably suffering from a mild case of shock. I called Dr. Jamison.

I quickly told him everything. The man's humanity was laudable because he said he would be coming to my aid immediately. He arrived within twenty-nine minutes. I walked him back outside to see the dead mother spider. He had no words, only total disbelief and horror. I broke the silence with a weak quip. "All this and the young-uns too, can be yours for the unbelievably low price of two million dollars."

"This offer is only good for today and just for you; otherwise, I'll be forced to call U C L A", I added. Dr. Jamison forced a weak smile and replied, "SOLD, American!" He looked at my wound and pronounced it non-lethal. I hoped that he was right but I wasn't quite convinced. Back in the house Dr. Jamison simultaneously worked on me and spoke on speaker phone to his boss at Cal-tech.

Both men were excited and agreed to acquiesce to my offer, but that I would need to be patient while they worked out the details.

I agreed but demanded that they both sign a contract to our agreement encumbering the university. They of course agreed. Then Dr. Jamison frightened me. He asked if I had any feeling around the wounded area. I realized that I felt nothing...nothing at all!

He called his boss back and told him to go to the lab to retrieve some sort of suction apparatus and a large glass cage.

Within thirty-two minutes Dr. Fallon arrived with all the materials.

The two men suctioned and cut a piece of flesh from me that I didn't even feel. They knew I would have to go to the hospital for at least stitches. We concocted a convincing story that we knew would satisfy the emergency staff. Then the two doctors went to see the dead spider. Dr. Fallon fell to his knees in disbelief. Dr. Jamison merely said, "I know Eric, but it's real"!

It was at that moment that I decided that I needed some insurance. I swung my cell phone out and took three silent pictures of the doctors with the beast.

I later got a great picture of Dr. Fallon putting the extracted egg sack into the glass cage. Dr. Fallon said, "We going to be studying this for years, surely until I retire". While they marveled at the dead freak of nature, I quickly typed out a little straight forward contract which included a non-disclosure clause for their protection. When presented they both signed it. Within the hour my nemesis was removed in a non-descript van by six football types wearing what appeared to be protective clothing.

It was finally decided that since my wound wasn't lethal, I would be cared for, not at the local hospital, but at the universities' medical clinic, because the wound seemed to be rapidly healing.

My first million-dollar check arrived within three weeks' time. The second would follow in approximately ten months. One would think that this would be the end of my story... far from it.

Changes were occurring within me. My hair returned and

in some areas on my body it had turned from gray back to a coal black. My appetite was infrequent, but when I did eat, I was ravenous. I could hear the faintest sounds, even those outside my bedroom window or even down the street.

My eyesight was perfect. I could see both far and near beyond what I used to see.

My stamina and strength were phenomenal. Spiderman? Hell, all I was missing was a flinging web. I laughed. I was sure that the toxin would eventually work its way through my body and I would return to being sub-par soon.

One morning about a week later I got up early to plant grass seeds on my front yard. While spreading seeds across the moistened fertilize soil, I remember thinking to myself, "I'm a millionaire now, I should be paying somebody to do this crap". In an instant my hair stood on end, and I heard panting. Simultaneously, my neighbor shouted, "Run brother man, run, there's a pack of wild dogs!" I wheeled around to see three dogs, one which was exceptionally large. They stopped to size me up.

"Run Brother!" I thought to myself, "I don't think so!" The big dog sprang forward far outpacing the rest. He lunged for my throat. Really bad idea. I caught him in midair with one hand closing my hand around his mouth, and wrapping my other arm around his front paws to avoid being scratched.

Then it happened, this irresistible compulsion to taste and consume its flesh. Without hesitation and in one dance-like motion, I saw myself bite through its neck and pulled out the majority of its arteries and veins.

The animal convulsed once from the violent trauma and instantly died. Quickly I stood up holding the limp corpse as a trophy to the other two animals that had stopped to witness with apprehension the goings on. Seeing the blood dripping from my mouth and their dead leader, they wisely decided that they wanted no part of me. They quickly did an about face, periodically looking over their shoulders to make sure that I wasn't in pursuit. My neighbor ran over to me and involuntarily recoiled in obvious sickening horror.

Regaining his composure, he finally said weakly: **"That was either the most courageous thing I've ever seen or the most vicious. I'm not quite sure which."** I reached for the garden hose and rinsed out my mouth, spitting out the last of my victim's flesh. I retorted: "I am in total agreement with what Malcolm X said. If I am to die, let it be even Stevens"! He further inquired, "You alright man? You, ok?"

"Yeah, I'm ok." I replied with a smile. "I just got to brush my teeth. And let's just keep this between you and me, ok? I don't want the Humane Society on my case." He laughed weakly and said: "ok!". His retreat was much like the two dogs because he too kept looking over his shoulder at me.

In truth, I was more than ok... I felt great. All of my senses were heightened and I felt fulfilled...even complete.

Within the next three weeks something would happen to change my life forever. One morning, as I was shaving my ever-hairy face, I saw that my face looked somewhat bloated. By the end of the day, it was so distorted that my jaws felt bloated. I ran to the bathroom mirror to see and feel what only could be described as mini fangs growing on top of my gum line pushing up my cheeks. Then it happened. The fangs began to emit the same pus-like substance that the spider had injected me with. I pressed a towel hard against my face causing the pus to escape into it. My face returned to normal, however, my body was spent! But the feeling was gratifying, indeed, almost exhilarating.

Had I undergone some sort of transformation? My thoughts raced wildly. What should I do? Was I dying? Was I contagious? I needed to talk to someone, Dr. Jamison, or Dr. Fallon. NO! NO! They would most certainly want to **STUDY ME… FOR YEARS**. I thought, "No, I don't think so!"

This scene of swelling and expulsion would repeat itself with regular periodicity. Every thirty days I had the need to relieve myself. The pus-like substance I learned was poisonous because it instantly killed my pet hamster. (**Don't ask!**)

Then it came to me. THIS DIDN'T HAVE TO BE A BAD THING! I LOVED Altadena. As I already told you, it's always been my town!

Over the years Altadena, like many American cities, has had its share of gang and drug vermin, while the justice system still remains ill equipped to handle the problems.

I now know that my "transformation" is permanent. And I AM TIRED of relieving myself in towels. Besides, it's about time that I give back to my beautiful Altadena as a millionaire and as an activist. I certainly have acquired a special power to help rid my beloved Altadena of some of its' undesirables.

My cheeks have begun to engorge themselves. A sure sign that it's about that time**. It's time to hunt!**

Mrs. Dinwitty's Herbal Tea

(a short story by m.i. williams jr.)

Mrs. Dinwitty had been a member of the Mount Olive Missionary Baptist Church for so long it was as if she was part of its history beyond what anyone could remember. Every Sunday morning and Wednesday night, you could set your watch by her precise arrival at church. It was sheer joy just to be around Mrs. Dinwitty.

She was definitely a people person, loving and generous to a fault. If someone was sick, she would drive to their home and offer them some of her chicken dumpling soup. For the members who just felt under the weather she would deliver some of her special hot herbal tea. Folks claimed that they didn't know what was in it, but if she ever decided to put a patent on it, she would put the Geritol people out of business.

Even the Pastor would go see her after an especially hard day to sit a spell with her and imbibe some of Mrs. Dinwitty special herbal tea. At one point, after church was over, folks had gotten Mrs. Dinwitty to bring some of her tea for the after service get together when the donuts and cookies were eaten in the conference hall.

This gathering was held in Sister Taylor's Young Adult Sunday school class.

Unfortunately, that soon had to come to a stop because of the overwhelming demand. The saints starting to push and shove in the Lord's house would never work. It was downright shameful! So, she quit making the tea publicly, again only serving it to those who were under the weather or sick and shut in.

It was in church that Mrs. Dinwitty's true grace and love came shining through. Often as she sang, she would gently touch the arm of a visitor as she went to and from the tithing box or she would unobtrusively stand and sing with the choir when the Spirit touched her. Though her voice had long passed its prime, her fervor for her faith just made you smile. She was always ready with a hug or a word of encouragement. It seemed she was a walking testament to the glory of God.

It was no wonder that when she became seriously ill one spring, that the whole church was deeply concerned. Sister Ellis had found her slumped down on the back porch, bloodied and dirtied, still wearing her gardening gloves.

She had come by to see her because Mrs. Dinwitty had missed prayer meeting.

Pastor wanted to come to the hospital himself but he had to leave for the annual Baptist conference that very night so he dispatched Sister Ellis to go in his stead and advised her to call him if there was anything seriously wrong. Call she did, as well as calling most of the church. The Pastor called his conference off...Mrs. Dinwitty needed his presence.

It was serious. Mrs. Dinwitty had suffered a severe concussion. The Church was in a state of spiritual malaise. The Deacon board and the Trustees had both proclaimed that they were soliciting prayers and that they both would be fasting for five days, so that their prayers would be more fervent in nature.

Sunday came and went and still Mrs. Dinwitty lay near death. Then it happened. Mrs. Dinwitty opened her eyes. At first, she seemed to be in a daze. She asked the nurse was she still in heaven. The church was ecstatic. There seemed to be a collective sigh of relief. Sadly, while Mrs. Dinwitty was unconscious the church lost a member, Brother Shifflett.

Since it seems that people always die in threes, everyone was glad that the church matriarch was spared by the Lord. She was understandably disoriented. In truth, she seemed to be changed. Her special effervescence had somehow been diminished. Everyone suspected that it would take time for her special light to return. Through it all, she had continued to praise the Lord. She even told all whoever would listen that she felt that she had been in the presence of the Lord, and that the Lord had given her a special mission.

Three weeks passed when Mrs. Dinwitty called the Pastor and asked that she be allowed to provide food and nourishment to the severely sick since she herself had been made better by the help of her fellow parishioners. The Pastor quickly agreed hoping that this service would further speed up her recovery. The Pastor did, however, insist that Mrs. Dinwitty take a traveling companion, just in case she had another "spell". She willingly agreed. Thank God that she would finally be able to serve the Lord in a meaningful way.

Mrs. Dinwitty's traveling companion was Sister Sarah Burks. Sister Burks was a retired registered nurse and her presence was reassuring to all concerned.

Two days after the agreement, Mrs. Dinwitty and Sister Burks went to see Brother Demus. Brother Demus had suffered with cancer for many years, his sight was also starting to fail badly and his present prognosis was not good. They would not be able to stay long because of his constant pain.

Mrs. Dinwitty had known Brother Demus and his late wife Zelda ever since they had moved from the Midwest. They were wonderful people. It was sad to see him suffer so. It wouldn't help his pain but she could give him some of her special chicken soup and herbal tea. He always liked that tea.

Today was no exception. He drank it down and instantly knew who had supplied it. "Is that you Sister Dinwitty"? "Yessiree, I'm here as the Lord commands". They both shared a laugh and a moment of quiet friendly familiarity. "God Bless you my sister".

They quietly departed, Mrs. Dinwitty feeling that she would probably not see her old friend again. She was right. Early the next morning Brother Demus had gone home to glory. Everyone at the church was glad to hear that he had died in his sleep, and that he was no longer in pain.

Mrs. Dinwitty was extremely pleased to know that she was able to bring some comfort to her old friend.

As fate would have it Mrs. Dinwitty was soon called upon by Phil and Doreen Hitchcox. Mother Hitchcox had a major stroke some years prior. Mrs. Dinwitty had known Evelyn

Hitchcox long before little Phil had been born. She had been a most socially active woman before her stroke. She too had visited the sick, made food baskets for the poor, and had led many a Women's Day program. She had labored long in the vineyard of the Lord. It was sad that she couldn't do for herself any longer.

Phil and Doreen were celebrating their 18th anniversary. They asked Mrs. Dinwitty to come sit with the elder Mrs. Hitchcox so they could go out and celebrate right. They really hadn't had time together since momma's stroke.

Quiet as it was kept, she had terrible psychological problems and had also become a heavy financial burden on them. But God would bless them for their loyalty and patience, especially when it came to Doreen. She had waited on her hand and foot like she was her very own mother.

Of course, Mrs. Dinwitty agreed to come. Sister Burks took her to the Hitchcox home, soup and tea in tow. Sister Burks was unable to stay due to a prior commitment but she was going to pick Mrs. Dinwitty up early the next morning.

That night Phil and Doreen went out and had the time of their lives. They had missed each other's company. One day they would have their lives back. While Phil and Doreen enjoyed themselves, Mrs. Dinwitty held an incessant one-way conversation with the oblivious Evelyn Hitchcox, and from time to time she managed to pour some of her herbal tea in her. She always loved that tea.

The next morning Mrs. Dinwitty went home with Sister Burks. They left Mother Hitchcox fast asleep. Little did anyone know that within a few hours Phil and Doreen Hitchcox would have their lives back. Dear Sister Hitchcox died of a massive heart attack. Just like folks said, death seemed to come in threes.

Later that evening, Sister Burks made a surprise visit to Mrs. Dinwitty.

"Ain't it kinda funny how so many people are just passin' away? Pastor mentioned it and I just got to thinking about it... it just seems odd." Just then Mrs. Dinwitty offered to pour tea.

"This batch is kinda experimental, it's made with wild strawberries." Sister Burks consented. She drank all the tea. It seemed to have a velvety quality about it although it was a tad pungent. Silence filled the room. Mrs. Dinwitty poured more tea for Sister Burks. Sister Burks took two more sips. "Sister Dinwitty, aren't you going to have some tea with me?" asked Sister Burks." "Why, yes child".

Uncharacteristically, Mrs. Dinwitty poured hot water over a common tea bag. Not knowing why, while having to clear her throat, Sister Burks blurted out a question: "Sister Dinwitty, tell me what did the Lord reveal to you as **your mission?**" Sister Dinwitty smiled ever so sweetly, and said: "The Lawd told me that suffering is not his plan, and the only thing that he wouldn't forgive is blasphemy of the Holy Spirit. And finally, since His will is perfect, his servant cannot be held accountable."

In that instant, the horrible truth had been revealed to Sister Burks. "**Mrs. Dinwitty**, **what have you done!!**?"

Unfeigned and maintaining an air of complete pleasantness, Mrs. Dinwitty replied: "Only the Lord's will." Just then Sister Burks felt her legs go numb as though they weren't there. Panic set in. She tried to stand up only to find herself on the kitchen floor, face up, staring at the smiling Mrs. Dinwitty.

"Oleander is a powerful and deadly drug, even in its natural state", said Mrs. Dinwitty. "Saturday, I harvested the Hawaiian Oleander that Sister Gertrude brought back from her Hawaiian vacation for me. And praise the Lawd, I finally got the mixture just right!" By now Sister Burks could only listen, because her vocal cords could no longer function. "Sister Girl I'm sorry, but I can't let **NOBODY stop the work of the Lawd**."

To say the least, the congregation was shocked at the news of Sister Sarah Burks' sudden death. Sometimes death even comes in fours. But everyone found comfort in knowing that she had been with the amazing Mrs. Dinwitty at the end. God Bless her.

She had comforted Brother Burks from the time the ambulance took Sister Burks from her house, through the time of the family repast. Mrs. Dinwitty even made a batch of her herbal tea for the entire guest party.

She even sent an extra special batch home with Sister Clinton for her terminally ill sister Clarice, with strict instructions that only Sister Clarice drink it because it was "kinda strong."

Praise the Lawd, Mrs. Dinwitty was back to normal. Yes, God bless Mrs. Dinwitty for her missions of mercy and continuing to do the Lawd's work.

A Washington State Love Story

(a short story by m.i. williams jr.)

Benjamin Calhoun Bedell was born a typical poor black child to Maddie and Ernest Bedell in Goodwater, Alabama. Ben was always big for his age and had always felt self-conscious about it. He was also quite dark-skinned, a fact that everyone seemed to have to constantly comment on. In truth, he was a handsome child, but people initially tended only to see his dark pigmentation.

Because of this, over time he began to keep to himself and retreated into the world of books. The first thing that impressed everyone about "Ben" was his ability to retain information about almost everything. This fact did not escape the notice of the young white librarian, Miss Meadows, who secretly encouraged him. She would often find time to interact with him, when no other whites were around. She also made it a point to let him check out books from the white section when no one else was looking.

Obviously, Ben excelled in school, so-much-so, that other students often sought him out to tutor them for pay.

In his senior year of high school Miss Meadows convinced the powers that be to hire Ben as a library assistant for a nominal wage.

Ben's dream was to go to college, but an early 1950's South was still not ready to accept a black academic no matter how smart he was.

Then one fateful day something happened to alter the very course of Ben's life. A young pretty white girl about Ben's age asked for his assistance. Ben aided her in locating her book, which necessitated going back into the deserted catacombs. As they were exiting, a stern voice boomed, "Hey boy, what do you think you're doing?" Stunned, Ben looked around to find himself surrounded by three red faced white boys standing in stature like football types. Quickly, the young girl came to Ben's defense. "Brad Riley, what are you talking about? Ben works here and was merely helping me!... and YOU ought to be ashamed of yourselves if you are suggesting anything improper that might impugn my reputation!"

This seemed to momentarily ease the tension. "Boy, don't let us catch you alone again with any of our women...ever!" Ben just stared beyond them. That evening Ben relayed what had happened to his father. Ernest Bedell knew all about the ways of the South... how something innocent could be turned into something life-threatening. Sure enough, within the week, that something happened.

It was actually only two days later, while walking home, that a car pulled up next to Ben and the same three white boys once again surrounded him. They had decided that they were going to teach this black bookworm a lesson or two. It would prove to be a painful lesson. First, Brad Riley swung a looping right fist that Ben caught in his open hand and twisted it behind him. He then pushed Brad into the next attacker causing both to hit the ground in a bloody heap. The last boy he merely backhanded onto the heap. Little did they suspect that Benjamin Calhoun Bedell, aka bookworm, was also extremely quick and exceedingly strong.

This last incident proved too much for the elder Bedell. He loved his only son far too much to allow the South to destroy him. It was then that he decided to take action. The elder Bedell, after consulting with his wife, went to Ben's school. He asked if Ben had enough credits to graduate immediately. Fortunately, he had more than the required credits. He asked that Ben's graduation papers be processed.

Within four days they arrived. During that time Ben was at home, he could no longer go to the library or even leave the house for fear of some sort of retaliation. Reluctantly, Ernest Bedell announced to his son that he was going to the army as an enlistee.

Initially the news saddened Ben, but his parents tried to soften his disappointment by explaining that in the military he would be able to travel, see the world, be educated, learn a trade, or even go to college up North. In any case, he would stay alive.

Fortunately, since the end of the war, things had begun to change in America. Truman had even integrated the armed services. The day that Ben left, he and his family were filled with mixed emotions. Ben was happy for the chance to see the world of his books, yet he was anxious.

Sensing his torment, his usually silent mother said, "All you need to take with you is Jesus, the talent that God gave you, and the love that we will always have for you, my son." With that they kissed him, waved good-bye, and watched the Greyhound Bus take him to Fort Lewis, in the far away state of Washington.

Ben's academic prowess and size did not escape his superiors at Fort Lewis either. After completing his basic training, unlike the other "colored boys", Ben was assigned to the all-white and prestigious 42Nd Military Police Brigade, which included officer's training school.

His assignments took him all over Europe. He made it a practice to visit the countryside and outlying areas of every country he visited. He enjoyed sightseeing, especially the churches and statues. In truth, traveling took his mind off the fact that he was quite lonely. Unlike most of the other men in his unit, Ben wasn't into deflowering the local girls and carousing. His buddies respected the fact that he was spiritually grounded. He became the unofficial chaplain of the group and he was known to keep the confidences of his peers.

When a buck private was reported A.W.O.L. on one occasion, it was Ben that the CO called to retrieve him discretely from the clutches of a Welch woman and her drunken brothers. Stateside Ben (who had become an officer), returned home occasionally to visit his extremely proud family.

As a dutiful son, he sent home part of his paycheck to help them out. It was appreciated but his mother would often scold him about sending so much. She insisted that he needed to be feathering his own nest so he could attract a pretty wife and give them some grandchildren. To this he would only laugh.

One fall day back in Washington as Ben was fishing on the outskirts of Fort Lewis, he observed a most curious sight. There appeared to be something rather large moving in the underbrush across the lake.

He couldn't quite make it out. He called but that seemed to frighten whatever it was.

What was worse, it seemed to be hobbling. He began to pursue. From time to time, he got a glimpse of something that appeared to walk upright but seemed odd.

As he steadily gained ground, the figure spoke. "Please leave me alone!" "You're trespassing!" "Leave!" It was definitely a woman's voice. Ben retorted, "You're hurt, let me help you!" By then Ben had caught up to her. Cowering, and hiding her face she pleaded, "No, stay away, please stay away." Ben tried to reassure her, "Ma am, I'm not going hurt you, honest."

Once again, she tried to escape but he pulled her back revealing her face. She had hair that came midway to her forehead and sideburns that covered most of her ears. The hair on her head was un-kept and was similar to fur. The back of her hands also was covered in hair.

Ben's heart was moved with a compassion that he had never felt before. He spoke gently. "My name is Ben Bedell. I'm a soldier at Fort Lewis. And it's my duty to serve any and every civilian of the United States, and today it is your turn." Ben waited for an answer that didn't seem to be coming. "Do you live around here? She nodded yes. "How did you hurt your leg?"

Still trying to hide her face, she answered, "I caught my boot and twisted my ankle on a river root...it'll be alright soon... just go, please." "NO! I'm sure I can carry you down to my jeep and get you to a hospital or doctor." This was not the right thing to say because she became hysterical.

Quickly Ben backed off. "OK, OK we won't do that! But I'm not leaving you here by yourself. Nightfall will be coming soon and wild critters will be out and it's going to get mighty cold. Let me take you home." A reluctant "OK" came, "but then you got to go and leave me be!" "Which way," he asked. "About a mile over that ridge to the east" was her reply.

They had walked for about a quarter mile when it became obvious that she couldn't walk any further. Without asking her permission he picked her up and carried her the remainder of the way. She was light as a feather. He could feel her shaking underneath her overcoat... she was exceedingly soft and warm.

As they reached the cabin, Ben was struck how large it was, even modern. As they entered the cabin, Ben looked for evidence of anyone else living with her. Sensing his thoughts, she said, "I live alone." As he put her down, she tumbled unto an old oversized sofa.

Then out of nowhere she blurted out: "Why are you being so nice to me? Can't you see that I'm a Freak?"

Ben was taken aback, but retorted, "No, I can only see that you are one of God's creatures and that in His eyes you are wonderfully made." "Then God must have a wonderful sense of humor," she scoffed. There was a long uncomfortable silence.

Ben inquired: "Are you hungry? I am." "You don't have to be nice to me or try to be noble. I really do appreciate your kindness but I can manage," she declared. It was now night and the fall air was bitter cold.

"Well, I'm just being me, Benjamin Calhoun Bedell. If I'm

going to make it back tonight, I'll need something warm in my gullet. What d'ya got that's quick and easy?"

Her reply came slowly. "I got some beans and franks if you like".

Ben replied: "I'd like that and I'll do the honors." The cabin was as neat and orderly as the camp commander's office.

As though reading his mind again, "My father was ex-military", she explained. Unexpectedly, it began to snow heavily. While eating, she and Ben began to talk. "I thought people from Washington were supposed to be neighborly, I don't even know your name."

She signed, "Even my name is a joke. It's Lovely...Lovely McGuire. Well, at least I was lovely until I was two years old."

She went on to explain that she had Hypertrichosis or Wolf Man Syndrome. She felt that she was kind of lucky because she didn't have hair overgrowth everywhere, but sparsely where people could see.

As a child she was taunted by the other children at school and even shunned by some teachers and concerned parents. Her parents, owning their family logging business, were later able to have her home schooled by private tutors. She further explained that before her parents' death, a trust fund was set up that supplied her every need by leasing out the lumber company and its facilities without giving up its ownership.

The irony was that many of the same children and families that had previously shunned her, unknowingly, now owed their very livelihood to her. Ben then told her his story. When he had finished, they both realized that it was near daylight.

Ben finally said, "I know that I have intruded on your solitude but I'd like to come back soon and check on you. Lovely,

I'm a pretty smart guy and I know that you couldn't have survived out here by yourself. Who in town is your contact for food and your essentials?"

"You are a policeman aren't you," came her reply. "Mrs. Cladder the storeowner and my mother were very close friends. She and her family bring me all my food and mail. It's the smallest but best general store in these parts." Ben: "Well, I noticed that you're running low on canned goods, maybe I could pick some up when I come back."

A doubting response of "Sure" quietly came back. "Tell me something Ben".

"Sure", said Ben. "Why would a handsome able body man like you want to come back?" Without hesitation, Ben said, "Maybe because I like talking to you". "I'll see you soon, ok?" A soft "Ok" came back.

Ben had only two hours to make it back to base on his two-day pass. On the way back home, he couldn't stop thinking about Lovely. She was bright, articulate, easy to talk to, and she seemed to be able to read his mind... that intrigued him most of all.

There seemed to be a bond between them, but why? Then it came to him like an epiphany. Lovely didn't want people to see her because of something nature had done to her. In Ben's world, white America didn't want to see him because he was a dark-skinned black male.

They both felt like outsiders in their own skins. Being on the outside makes one become more reflective and more guarded. Outsiders keep to themselves. Only outsiders see the inward beauty and depth of each other. He had really felt at ease with her...and she was so soft and warm. He had to see her again and soon. Funny, he had never understood why soldiers went A.W.O.L ...until now. He had to see her again, no matter what.

The next day he wrote Lovely a letter and sent it to the small general store. In it he sent a picture of himself and his parents along with some of his favorite scriptures. To his surprise she sent him a letter saying that her foot was much better and that she hoped that she would see him soon. She also included a scripture from Jesus that read: When you do it for the least of these, you have done it for me. This was Ben's most favorite scripture. Not wanting to be demeaning, he hadn't sent this, his favorite scripture...but how did she know?

The next weekend Ben maneuvered a forty-eight-hour pass. He went directly to the small general store and purchased fun food for the weekend. Mrs. Cladder was well into her seventies but was still very sharp. She knew who he had to be. "Well young man, I can tell by your accent that you're not from around these parts." Ben laughed and retorted, "They also don't grow as dark as me in these parts either!"

She snickered. Quietly she asked, "Are you going to visit with my nocturnal friend on the mountain?"

"Yes ma'am, I am." "You're one of them military police aren't ya?" "Yes ma'am, how did you know?" "You're bigger and stronger than most. I'm also hoping that you're kinder than most too. Lord knows that girl has suffered enough in her life." Ben smiled, then said: "What can I do to show her a good time? Mrs. Cladder paused and thought for a moment. "Maybe I could arrange a private movie for ya'll late tomorrow night. Milt Taylor is the manager and he owes me a big favor." "Are you sure?" Ben asked. "Yeah, just come around midnight.

Truth be told, I don't think Lovely has ever been in a movie house."

"We'll be there!" Ben said excitedly.

Ben arrived at Lovely's out of breath. The groceries and the steep climb had winded him. To his surprise, Lovely was wearing a soft cotton plaid shirt. She was no longer trying to hide her face or her hands. But her hair was brushed to the side, and there was a distinct fragrance of perfume in the air. And she had made dinner.

"You said you were coming today so I made us some supper." They ate and made small talk.

Little did Lovely know that Ben had mentally rehearsed a script about going to the movies.

Ben: "Tell me, why don't you have a T.V.?"

Lovely: "The reception is bad, or at least it used to be when I was little, never thought about it. I keep myself busy in my garden. I write children books, I paint, listen to the radio, I walk, I knit."

Ben: "So, you don't get out much, huh?"

Lovely: "No, Ben, you know I don't? Where's this conversation going?"

Ben: "Well, I've spoken to your friend Mrs. Cladder. I think she likes me. She says if I bring you to the movie house at midnight tomorrow, she will guarantee that we could have a private movie showing just for us. Some guy called Milt Taylor is going to arrange it."

Lovely: "Milt Taylor was one of the bastards that teased me when I was little!"

Ben: "This isn't about Milt Taylor. This is about me taking you on a date! Besides Lovely, people and things change over time."

Lovely: "Let me think about it Ben, ok?"

Ben: "Sure", he replied. Ben didn't push it. The rest of the night was filled with Scrabble and singing along with the radio.

Then Lovely proclaimed that she was tired and showed Ben to his room. Without warning Ben kissed her on the cheek. She stood there in shock. Lovely: "Why did you do that?" Ben whispered: "I think you know why."

Lovely: "I'm glad you came to my state of Washington Ben Bedell."

Ben: "I wasn't so sure I had made the right decision until I met you."

Lovely: "My mother would say of you: You're a **DIFFERONT** kind of duck." Ben sensing what she meant said, "Yeah, I've always felt awkward in my skin, ***Differont***."

"Why", she asked. "You're so big and strong and handsome." "Handsome! That's a new one!" he exclaimed.

Lovely: "Enough of your false modesty, you know that your gorgeous. I've seen the hunters in the area and none compare to you. What I want to know is why you would want to bother with someone like me?"

Ben: "Lovely, being with you is in no way a bother, and I haven't found anyone I wanted to be with until now. Your hair can't cover up your beautiful nature, your honesty, your intelligence, and your warm personality. You're easy to be with because you're real." With those earnest words Lovely began to softly cry. Ben went to her and softly held her close.

Lovely: "Well Ben Bedell, I'm yours if you want me." Ben quickly pronounced, "I do, I want you." Then Lovely said: "Ben, I know that you can't marry me. All I ask is that you treat me with respect. I know that a man needs to be able to socialize with his wife, and lead some kind of normal life. I can never have that kind of life. But I'll give you all that I am able, starting with going to that movie."

Ben was at first speechless, but then he managed to say: "Lovely, my momma once told me that God made the earth curved so we couldn't see too far down the road. Let's just start walking down this road together and see what God has in store for us."

Lovely agreed with a meek: "OK." Since I'm not quite ready for you to see all of me yet, I'm going to my bedroom." Ben grasped for words: "I didn't expect you to...What I meant to say is...." Lovely kissed Ben on his cheek and said: "I was only teasing you. Good night, Ben."

The next morning Ben awoke to the smells of hickory smoked bacon and Colombian coffee. Lovely had gone all out. The food was sumptuous. She was a darn good cook. Again, as if reading his mind: "My mother needed to keep my occupied so she taught me how to cook. Sometimes we'd fix meals for some of the loggers and workers.

The rest of the day was spent with Lovely showing Ben around her mountain home. Periodically she stopped to compose herself as she allowed herself to reminiscence on the happy times that she enjoyed with her parents.

Since Lovely had been forced to be sequestered, her parents did the same. Her mother spoke only with her friend Mrs. Cladder and the private tutors. Father interacted generally with the public, but he felt more comfortable with the loggers and workers. The property was vast; not even an eighth of it had been worked in all the years of the logging operations. The wind is bitter in Washington State especially in the winter. They returned to the cabin early to escape the oncoming cold. Lovely announced that supper would be light since they were going to be out late going to the movie.

"What will we be seeing?" she inquired. Ben: "I think it's called, ***My Fair Lady*** or something like that."

Lovely: "Good, just as long as it's not one of those wolf man movies!" They both laughed simultaneously.

They waited until the sun was nearly down to drive to the movies in the closed air army jeep. Ben, sensing her apprehension said, "We will wait to go in at the last minute, and I'll go find a secluded spot."

She smiled and retorted, "Now who's the mind reader?" Ben did exactly as he said. They entered the movie from the side exit door.

The attendant opened the door and said, "Hello Lovely, it's been a long time". Lovely looked up to see the unmistakable face of one of her childhood tormentors, Milt Taylor.

"I'm part owner and manager of the theater", he said. "You know you don't have to hide out in your mountain home anymore Lovely. Everybody knows you're up there...and we've all grown up a lot from the old days. Lovely said nothing.

Milt went on: "As for me, I hope one day you can forgive that brat-ass kid that teased you so long ago. I've come to know a little of how you felt. I got a boy with severe learning disabilities and life's been kind of hard on him too. Well, come on in and see the show."

Slowly and sincerely, Lovely looked up and said, "I can

and I do forgive you". Wiping heartfelt tears from his eyes, Milt responded: "Thanks Lovely, I really needed to hear that."

While watching the movie, Lovely felt like the weight of a heavy and unwarranted shame had been lifted from her. For the first time since being with her parents, she didn't feel like a freak. She rested her head on Ben's broad shoulder. It felt good...it felt reassuring. Ben felt it too.

She felt so warm to him. Then, as if on cue, Lovely chimed in, "You feel warm too." She wondered if this feeling would last. Then as if by telepathy, Ben said, "Don't worry. I think I've figured out how to be together forever."

It was settled, and they both knew it. So, when they kissed, it was more like a wedding kiss than their very first one. Ben instantly recognized it as true love for the second time in his life.

The next day Ben reported back to the base. His first stop was to the company chaplain. After hearing the full story, he agreed to help Ben work his plan, but on one condition. That condition was that he would perform the nuptials. Ben eagerly agreed. Next was a call to the Camp CO.

The CO listened intently but without any expression or hint as to his thinking. He then excused Ben and advised him that he would talk further with him later. This surprised Ben because he always thought that the CO kinda liked him.

The next morning new orders were posted. His unit was being dispatched to Guam. Then, an unusual change in protocol occurred. The name of every man dispatched to Guam was listed. Every name was there except Ben's name. Ben was nervous...no, downright scared. What was going on?

Had the CO decided against him? He loved Lovely. Perhaps he was against interracial marriage.

He would not leave her! He would have to resign. Resignation was the only course of action.

The next day, with his resignation in his pocket, Ben requested to see the CO. The permission was denied. So, Ben left the resignation envelop with the CO's secretary. The very next day, Ben was summoned to the CO's headquarters. This time it was the CO that scripted the scene to follow.

Camp CO: "Mr. Bedell, I have reviewed your file and see that there are about eleven months before you are to reenlist or be honorably discharged. I've always respected you for your high standards of excellence and morals. I expect you to continue to adhere to those high standards. I would sincerely hate to lose a man of your caliber, but if you do opt out of the service, I know that wherever you serve you will be an asset. Take that little town you spoke of, DuPont. It's come to my attention that in about eleven months the sheriff there is due to retire. That means that everybody will move up a notch and they'll be needing a good man. I'm also told that a man of your background would be snapped up. You think you could hold out eleven months and police this camp if you weren't dispatched elsewhere?"

BEN: "Oh yes Sir! I could certainly do that sir!"

Camp CO: "I was hoping that you said that. Besides, planning a decent wedding takes some time, doesn't it soldier?"

Ben: "Yes Sir, it does Sir!"

Camp CO: "Oh, by the way, my secretary said you accidentally dropped this envelop the other day. Why don't you take it?"

Ben: "Yes SIR!"

Camp CO: "Good luck, soldier. Dismissed."

BEN: "Yes Sir." Ben was overwhelmed. He couldn't wait to tell Lovely. Then he stopped. He had never REALLY asked Lovely to marry him. "What a Jerk!" he thought to himself. He decided to correct that oversight the following week. The next week wasn't necessary, because the chaplain came through with another emergency forty-eight-hour pass with the CO's stamp on it!

Ben's head was bombarded with things to do. He had to tell his parents. They would probably be surprised about Lovely but happy for him. Next, he would get Lovely to install a phone, this driving was insane. He would stop by the sheriff's office and fill out a job application to have it on file.

Foremost, he would stop by a jeweler in Tacoma, buy a beautiful engagement ring and then ask Lovely to be his wife. Maybe he had the wrong order but he would get it all done somehow. The ring was an Empress design made with platinum. He wasn't sure about the size but he would resize it later if needed.

With ring in tow, Ben reached the cabin. Without knocking he eagerly let himself in.

There was Lovely standing in the middle of the room completely nude. She had removed all the hair from her face and hands and was finishing shaving the nape of her neck. She was gorgeous from head to toe. She was quite pale from always hiding herself with bulky clothes, and except for the red areas from the shaved areas, she was something out of the movies.

"You're not supposed to be here until next weekend," she managed to say while grabbing for a towel that wasn't able to hide her wonderfully curvaceous frame. After realizing how fruitless her efforts to hide were, she came over to Ben and asked: "Well, do you like what you see?"

Ben responded, "Oh yeah! Lordy, Please just don't let me go blind NOW!!He wanted to make her his right then, but then she said: "Good, but you'll just have to wait a little longer, I'm still not quite ready yet." "I know, said Ben, but let's start the clock ticking." With that he pulled out the ring. Lovely threw the towel down and reached for the ring. "Lovely McGuire, would you do me the honor of becoming this unworthy man's wife?" he asked.

As big tears came streaming down her face and onto her luscious breasts, she screamed over and over again: **"YES, YES, YES."**

Ben sighed: "Thank you my darling. Now PLEASE go put some clothes on so I can retrieve some sense of my Christianity and tell you all the great news." Lovely dashed off and returned later, this time without the red blotches on her face.

Once again reading his thoughts she replied: "Mrs. Cladder brought some stuff called a depilatory that temporarily removes hair. I was told by a doctor that repeated hair removal in some cases have lessened some of the less hairy areas. I never tried before because I never saw any need to before now... before you. She also brought me some thick makeup. Does it look ok?"

Ben: "Lovely, it looks terrific. But you know that it doesn't matter to me."

Lovely: "I know it doesn't, but now it matters to me, especially when we're out in public. I want to be the best Mrs. Benjamin Calhoun Bedell that I can be." Holding her warmly, it was Ben's turn to cry.

It seemed that what was to have been a small intimate wedding ended up being the town's social event of the year. Ben's entire platoon was there including the CO and his staff. Ben's parents were of course present. His father was his best man. His mother looked on incessantly wiping away tears of joy. Mrs. Cladder was of course, the official wedding planner.

Under the imposing backdrop of Mount Rainier, the two were wed, with the coup de grace being Milt Taylor giving the bride away. Of course, there were the curious who came out to see the famous hairy woman who wasn't all that hairy. Others had come to see the new big black sheriff deputy that she was going to marry. Their genuine love and respect for one another could be felt more than seen. And when they kissed, everyone knew they were witnessing a true Washington State love story.

Made in the USA
Coppell, TX
12 March 2026

73661162R00069